Six-foot plus, blond Adonis types did not ask Alex on dates. So when JJ Vanzant did just that, it made her suspicious and snippy. What did he—in all his sexy glory—want with a run-down single mother of two who was currently unemployed? What she needed was a job, not a fling. Unfortunately, the best and only job available was at his private detective agency. His ego would just have to take the rejection because she'd been hired and was going nowhere.

JJ didn't know if he'd been blessed or cursed when Alex showed up in his office, but she couldn't stay there. So his friend, Nance, was tasked with finding her another job. Meanwhile, all he had to do was keep his hands off her . . . which proved damn near impossible. In the time it takes for him to fall for the dark-haired minx, he would have to help her keep custody of her two adorable boys. But what will happen if she doesn't need him anymore? Will his heart get broken like it was when he was a child?

What JJ Wants
Copyright © 2019 Quinn K Clancy and Mary Clancy
ISBN: 978-1-4874-2224-0
Cover art by Martine Jardin

Published by eXtasy Books Inc or
Devine Destinies, an imprint of eXtasy Books Inc

Look for us online at:
www.eXtasybooks.com or www.devinedestinies.com

What JJ Wants
Triple Threat Book 2

By

Quinn K Clancy and Mary Clancy

DEDICATION

For our brothers, Raymond and Norm, as well as our father, Gerald.

PROLOGUE

JJ stepped into the kitchen of Viv Wilder's home and faltered momentarily at the sight of a pretty brunette rinsing dishes at the sink. With the water running to mask the sound of his footsteps, he was able to study her thoroughly before she noticed his presence. She was petite, about five-five, and he figured she'd weigh no more than a hundred pounds sopping wet. Her coal-black hair was curly and tumbled just past narrow shoulders.

His gaze wandered to a curvy bottom encased in well-worn jeans, perhaps not as curvy as he suspected it would be if she gained a little weight. She appeared too slim even for such a small person, her fine bone structure a tad too pronounced in the glimpse he'd been given of her delicate wrists as she twisted a cup under cascading water.

The sweatshirt bagging haphazardly around her hips was faded to a dull navy, its material having obviously seen the inside of a washing machine more times than it was meant to.

His detailed perusal was threatened to be cut short when she shut off the tap and dried her hands on a towel. She had turned slightly toward him, and he traced her profile with an avid gaze. Her brow was creased in concentration, and her finely arched eyebrow twitched as it seemed to be tickled by a stray ringlet. Her long, dark lashes were lowered against high cheekbones that were a touch too prominent in her lovely face.

Desire shot through him when she unconsciously wet almost-red lips, her pink tongue tracing the fullness of the lower one. Her mouth would be soft to kiss and generous in a smile, but he had a feeling she rarely laughed.

He struggled to contain his shocking arousal, glad that his bulging fly was hidden by his own shapeless sweatshirt. He'd been months without female companionship, which was the only explanation for this sudden itch to grab a complete stranger and kiss the living daylights out of her.

Petite brunettes were not his type. He liked his women blonde and long in the leg. Or he had, until this enchanting entity turned the full force of her gaze on him and he realized what he'd been missing.

She took a step back and gripped the edge of the counter. The most beautiful brown eyes JJ had ever seen widened in surprise, thickly fringed with black lashes. He could drown in those eyes.

JJ snapped out of his trance when she blinked, clearing his throat to let some air pass. He set his load down on the table and remembered why he was there.

"Sorry to startle you," he said gruffly. "I'm installing Viv's security system." He waved a big hand at the box he'd carried in before shoving it through his blond hair. Was he ever nervous around women? *No.* He kicked himself for acting like a schoolboy.

"Oh," said the vision, her shoulders relaxing. "You're JJ Vanzant, the private investigator." She extended a small hand which was engulfed in his. "I'm Alex Manning. I live up the street."

Dumbly, he nodded and reluctantly released her. "Nice to meet you," his mouth obediently told her. "I'll try not to get in your way while I'm here."

"That's fine. I'm about ready to leave anyway." Her lips quirked into a semblance of a smile, and he was fascinated by it. Alex shuffled her feet awkwardly. "You're staring."

"I'm sorry," he mumbled, heat racing up his neck. "You're quite beautiful." He darted his attention to her ring finger, relieved to find it bare.

Alex's hand fluttered to her hair, her lips parting on a stunned gasp. "That's very polite of you, considering the state I'm in."

"I'm not being polite. In fact," he swallowed, not believing his nerve, "I was wondering if you're not too busy this weekend—maybe you'd like to go out somewhere?"

Something in her expression changed, hardened. "You're joking, right?"

"Certainly not." He was confused by her reaction, her stance becoming defensive as she folded thin arms. It was only a casual invitation, but she glared a fair bit over it. Mentally, he whistled, thinking it was a good thing she didn't know what was happening in the nether regions of his anatomy. She'd likely deck him.

"I am busy, actually." She grabbed her denim jacket and hurriedly shrugged into it as Viv entered the room.

Viv introduced her to JJ's university buddy, Jonas Mackenzie, before Alex scuttled out the back door claiming she had to rush home to her sick mother.

Whew! You'll have to brush up on your social skills, Vanzant.

That was the oddest reaction he'd garnered from a woman in his adult life. Usually, he got a little consideration on the matter before being turned down. He doubted her mother was ill at all. His boldness must have spooked her into fibbing that excuse and making tracks.

Viv was still frowning worriedly after seeing Jonas off to work. JJ had sensed his friend was becoming involved with the striking blonde woman, an association he applauded wholeheartedly.

After telling Viv he may have insulted her friend by asking her out, he proceeded to set a sensor on the window casing. His gaze rested on the closed gate outside that Alex had disappeared through, and he grimly wondered what he'd said to upset her. Of course, perhaps she just found his interest too forward and downright rude, as he'd assumed — or maybe *he* wasn't *her* type at all.

"She's had a rough time of it lately." Viv's soothing tone placated his bruised ego somewhat, allowing him to get back to what he was doing.

Unfortunately, his work only distracted him for so long and then he was left with the puzzle of Alex Manning to ponder all that day, and several days after, those haunted brown eyes following him everywhere he went.

CHAPTER ONE

Why, oh *why* had she agreed to be Viv's maid of honor? Alex stood stiffly at her friend's side clutching a tiny bouquet of pink roses and baby's breath nervously. Dressed in her pale-blue pant suit, she felt like a midget next to the blushing bride's statuesque radiance. Her hands were sweating, and she was sure the elegant upswept hairdo that had been expertly fashioned at a salon that morning would explode from its pins any second into a riotous cloud of black.

Of course, to make matters worse, one of the groomsmen had to be that irritating blond Adonis from the kitchen incident. The one who'd taken one good gawk at her washed-out self and decided to offer a pity date.

Viv had been having problems with an unwanted would-be suitor and had opted to have an alarm system installed. One look at the man responsible for the task, and Alex knew he spelled trouble. She'd removed herself from his company as fast as her legs would carry her, fearful that those magical blue eyes would have her thinking he was actually serious about having dinner together.

"Dearly Beloved," intoned the minister, "we are gathered here today . . ."

As if JJ Vanzant of the broad shoulders and lean-hipped swagger would ever be interested in a skinny, perpetually exhausted, unemployed, widowed mother of two.

" . . . to join this couple in holy matrimony."

She might be only twenty-seven, but Alex had no illusions about her attractiveness to men. Her husband had made sure of that long before he'd died.

Focusing on her friends, Vivian and Jonas, she continued to ignore the sapphire gaze that had locked on to her when she'd arrived at the Mackenzie estate.

"Do you, Jonas . . ."

The expression on the groom's face caught Alex's attention. The big, gruff redhead stared solemnly into the eyes of the woman he adored, pledging his eternal love. A watery smile trembled on Viv's lips as she answered in kind.

"By the power vested in me . . ."

Alex blinked away a tear as they kissed and the small group of family and friends in the solarium erupted in applause. She glanced up and immediately regretted it when she encountered JJ's intense stare.

"Now, since this is our belated Thanksgiving," Eleuthera Mackenzie announced to the room at large, "we shall adjourn to the dining room for a feast and an absolutely stunning cake prepared by Cook." She dabbed her eyes once more before embracing her son and his new wife.

Jonas had been near-fatally wounded in early October, and no one had really felt like celebrating the holiday until he'd recovered. The postponed event then became an opportunity for him to surprise Viv with an impromptu ceremony—once he'd convinced his somewhat recalcitrant love that it was meant to be.

Alex stood chatting with Cassandra and Caroline, Viv's twin cousins from Bay de Chance, as the rest of the Kincaid clan filed out behind their hostess. The large family had come down to St. John's for the surprise wedding at a moment's notice, more than happy to see their adopted sibling tie the knot.

The best man, Jonas' uncle Michael, and the other groomsman, Steven Kincaid, escorted the twins out. Alex reluctantly gave her arm to JJ and followed in silence, thinking somehow that he'd smoothly maneuvered it so that the best man was paired with the wrong woman. She didn't point out the untraditional match as it would probably draw awkward attention.

"Boisterous bunch, aren't they?" JJ murmured.

"Mmm-hmm."

"You look lovely, by the way." He slid her a sideways glance. "Or am I not allowed to say that?"

Stiffly, she muttered, "You can say whatever you like."

"Well, I seem to recall the last time I tried to pay you a compliment you nearly snapped my head off."

"I did not snap, and could you pick up the pace a bit? The way you're walking, we'll never make it to the dining room door before Christmas." Alex tried pulling her arm free, but he tightened his hold.

"Tsk, tsk, Mrs. Manning. Aren't we a little touchy for such a joyous event?"

Relenting, she said, "It's *Alex*, and I don't use the *Mrs.* anymore."

She knew he was watching her intently but said nothing more as they joined the others. Grateful when he released her arm, she left him to find her seat, only to realize she'd been placed next to the bothersome man at the head table. Another cagey move, but then she chided herself for being paranoid.

"Relax, will you? I'm perfectly aware that you dislike my company," JJ grimly informed her. "Just so you don't have a heart attack, I should probably warn you that we'll be expected to dance later. Together," he tacked on with a shameless grin that made his dimples so deep they were more like grooves in his cheeks.

No man had any right to look so good. She tried not to notice how he settled his six-foot frame in the chair beside her with a grace that was reminiscent of a cat. Or that his cologne was a subtle woodsy scent that she found very appealing. Or that his tux fit him to absolute masculine perfection. Or that his hair curled close to his well-formed head and stayed obediently off his brow. She tried not to notice—and failed.

Alex also fell short of feeling completely at ease among this group of people—she, an out-of-work secretary with two young sons to feed while subsisting on public aid. Thankfully, the only person there who knew of her dire financial situation was Viv, who had befriended her while they worked on their neighborhood breakfast program. Alex had been faintly ashamed of having to avail of charity, but Hank and Billy needed the extra nourishment to stay healthy and do well in school. She felt badly enough about mooching off her elderly parents by living with them. She couldn't expect them to dole out precious retirement income to their single daughter.

If only she hadn't contracted that awful flu virus a few months back and subsequently lost her job. Heck, she'd never have been able to attend the wedding if Eleuthera Mackenzie hadn't insisted on picking up the tab for the bridesmaids' outfits.

Then there was Darryl's credit card debt. Her husband had been dead for two years, but Alex was still up to her neck in overdue payments for his habit. Too bad he'd gambled away all of their savings before he'd gotten sick. Swallowing bitterly, she chastised herself for the selfish thought. The man was gone, after all.

The sound of utensils tapping on crystal brought Alex out of her reverie, and she couldn't help smiling as the happy couple stood and kissed, cheered on by hoots and wolf whistles.

"Make your teeth ache?" a deep voice rumbled in her ear.

Startled, she frowned at JJ. "What?"

"All that sweetness and happy-ever-after stuff," he clarified, nodding at Jonas and Viv. "I never went for it myself."

"No, your type wouldn't." After that dampening statement, she went back to eating her cake.

"What exactly does that mean? *Your type*?"

"The footloose, carefree, chase-anything-in-a-skirt type." Alex knew she was baiting him, perhaps unfairly. He *was* a successful PI with his own firm—he must be responsible some of the time. As for the skirts, well, she'd let that stand. It was plain that her dismissal of a date with him had rankled—that was most assuredly the reason behind him getting in her face now.

"I suppose you're all for that commitment tripe," JJ grumbled after such a long pause that she'd been on the verge of apologizing for her rudeness.

"As a matter of fact, I am, when two people are right for each other."

Just because it didn't work out for me doesn't mean it can't for them.

Something flickered in his eyes when she looked at him.

"I'm sorry, I forget you're a widow. That was insensitive." He seemed so sincere that Alex could only turn back to her plate without saying anything, certainly not that her own dream had turned to dust.

It was no business of his that her marriage had been one disappointment after another until she'd finally had enough. She refused to justify her feelings about relationships or anything else to calm his ruffled feathers. The man was simply toying with her, trying to aggravate her as much as possible while she had to endure his company for the sake of mutual friends.

Certain that JJ would grow bored with it, she finished the cake and pretended to be very interested in the bubbles in her glass of champagne.

Damn! He mentally kicked himself. *You had to bring up something that obviously caused her great pain. Way to go, you jerk!*

JJ sighed and gulped from his wineglass. If the way she'd turned from him was any indication, he'd put his foot in it good. It wasn't bad enough to give her the impression that he had little respect or admiration for the sanctity of marriage, he had to remind her of her loss. It was apparent she still had feelings for her dead husband or she wouldn't have flinched like that.

Damn and double damn.

Well, at least he'd gotten her attention. He'd become heartily sick of being ignored by the dark-haired vixen. If he hadn't noticed her sneaking those looks at him now and then, he'd accept that she wasn't interested.

How many times since that morning at Viv's had he wished he could go back and undo whatever it was he did to offend her in the first place? Grief, he'd only asked her out! He was good company and far from over the hill, although his thirty-five-year-old body had not craved any female *companionship* for several months.

It wasn't as if he'd never been turned down. It happened seldom but it had happened. Normally, he'd shrug it off and go on about his business, but even weeks after meeting Alex he had trouble concentrating without having an image of her flash through his memory at odd moments. She was disrupting his work and his pitiful social life. The one date he'd had in months had seemed too blonde, too brassy, too not Alex Manning. He'd taken the woman to her place and hugged her goodnight—*hugged her, for God's sake, and left her at the door!*

He'd been in his glee to learn she was Viv's maid of honor, thinking he'd finagle a dance or two at the reception. How pathetic. Here he was, a grown man with his own thriving company, trying desperately not to peek down the cleavage of this gorgeous, stubborn woman.

Sighing again, he drained his glass.

Once the remnants of the meal had been cleared, the waiters that had been hired by Eleuthera efficiently transformed the great dining room into a softly lit ballroom. Tables were arranged just so to allow space for dancing, candles placed strategically to enhance the romantic mood.

Mr. and Mrs. Mackenzie took to the floor for the traditional first waltz. Jonas' fiery red head bent close to his bride's, and he gently brushed his lips over hers.

JJ stood off to one side in the semi-darkness and fought a pang of envy as he witnessed the happy couple's embrace. His friend deserved to find contentment with a good woman and get started on raising a family.

It had always seemed inevitable to JJ that his college buddies, Jonas, and Viv's cousin, Steven Kincaid, would one day find that someone special to share their lives. While Steven had not yet followed the redhead in the pursuit of happiness, JJ was certain it would eventually come to pass.

His friends had been brought up in the secure structure of a family and found comfort in the knowledge that their relatives would support them in times both good and bad, unlike the orphan JJ somehow sensed he would always be. True, he had his longtime companions who were as close as brothers to him, but the feeling of being disconnected had stayed with him ever since his alcoholic mother had dumped him on the steps of an orphanage without bothering to sign the papers necessary for him to be legally adopted. Not that many people had been looking to adopt an eight-year-old, moody little boy with a penchant for finding trouble.

He jiggled the ice in his empty glass and decided against a refill as he watched the couple separate, Jonas leading his mother to the floor while Viv took her Uncle Jon's hand.

Loneliness swept over him, and he automatically stepped

farther into the shadows, hoping his presence would go un-noticed as he indulged in old and painful memories—the nuns with their falsely bright smiles telling him they'd found a new foster home, one of his foster mothers locking him in a closet for so long that he'd wet his pants at the ripe old age of eleven, having to bite the arm of his second foster father so he'd be sent back to the orphanage and not have to worry that the pervert would put his slimy hands on him.

Of course, they hadn't all been bad. Most had treated him well, but they just didn't think of him as their child. He'd learned to maintain a certain distance because he soon real-ized that eventually he'd have to leave. No, family for JJ was just something he'd come to accept was not in the cards.

Lost in the past, he didn't notice the music change until she stood before him and offered her hand. Alex's eyes, for the first time since he'd stumbled upon her in Viv's kitchen, had lost their haunted look and were glowing softly, large and dark and possessing a light that sparked a response in his soul. Hope.

"I think this is where we're supposed to dance," she whispered, wiggling her fingers at him.

Now, what had made her change her attitude so radically and so fast? Twenty minutes ago, she'd treated him like the lowest on the totem pole. *Oh well, why question it?*

Shoving back the reminders of his past, JJ placed his glass on a table and fitted his palm against hers as she led him to-ward the music.

Weddings always had this effect on her. Just the simple act of watching two people so devoted to each other created an illusion of serenity in her own jumbled life. Problems seemed insignificant for a little while, and she got caught up in the moment. There were no resumes to mail, no bills to pay, no worries whatsoever.

Apparently, the sight of matrimonial bliss did not affect JJ Vanzant the same way. She'd gotten a glimpse of him practically hidden behind a darkened fern, staring into his glass with a too-somber expression on his face. His broad shoulders had risen and fallen slowly, as if resettling an invisible burden. For long minutes she'd watched before her feet made the decision to walk over to him.

Now, as one big hand rested in the small of her back and the other cradled hers against his chest, she wondered if giving in to the urge to wipe that troubled look away had been wise. His cologne mingled with another, more elusive scent that she knew was distinctly his—a bit spicy and very sensual. Without thinking, she edged closer, the top of her head brushing his chin. He leaned down and pressed his cheek to hers, and she knew she ought to back off. After all, she'd spent the entire evening trying to stay out of his way, so this was definitely sending the wrong signal. She considered putting some distance between his slightly rougher cheek and hers, but her traitorous face would not cooperate. This really wasn't wise.

JJ was careful of her, his touch almost tender as they swayed to the love song being played by the string quartet. Alex fancied he was very respectful of her smaller, less substantial frame. Skinny, she ruefully corrected. She'd lost a lot of weight while she'd been ill and hadn't gained much of it back. Her wrists were too thin, and her ribs were too prominent to anyone with a mind to examine them. Thankfully, no one had.

She closed her drooping lids and sighed. Who was she kidding anyway? A whiff of the man was all she could afford with so much on her plate—and JJ was way out of her league. No handsome, successful, fun-loving guy in his right mind would take on a relationship with someone who carried a load as big as hers. Certainly not one who, by his own earlier admission, was commitment-shy.

"Song's over." JJ's arms remained around her. "Want another, or is one dance all you can stomach with me?"

"I don't mind one more—but I'll probably fall asleep on you."

He laughed softly and tucked her head under his chin. "I'll chance it."

So they stayed that way until Steven Kincaid asked to cut in. The glare JJ sent him was ignored with a grin, and he glided with Alex across the floor.

The reception lasted almost 'til midnight, everyone waltzing with everyone else. Finally, the long-awaited moment for the tossing of the bouquet and garter arrived.

Alex was dragged into the laughing group of single women, stunned when the bride threw the rose blooms directly at her. It *thunked* on her chest, and she automatically put her hands up to save the lovely creation from crashing to the floor. The other guests roared in appreciation and shouted for the groom to get rid of the scrap of *something blue* in his hand, and her face burned.

Jonas flipped the garter over his shoulder in the opposite direction of where the bachelors had gathered, seemingly oblivious to the fact that JJ had deliberately held himself apart from the rest. The blond man was startled to find the lacy thing on his head and grinned sassily as he plucked it from its resting place.

Grateful that she was wearing pants, Alex complied with tradition, and she extended her leg for JJ to do the honors. The suit was fashionably loose, however, which enabled him to slide the fabric above her knee. And was it just her imagination, or did those warm hands linger unnecessarily on her bare skin?

Disregarding her flaming embarrassment, he rose and

gallantly brought her hand to his lips, blue gaze burning into hers amid more cheers. She scowled back, not comfortable at all with the predatory gleam there.

"Lighten up, Alex. I don't bite." He smiled down at her and added, "Well, not very hard and only in private." Wiggling thick eyebrows, he leered comically.

"Forget it, Romeo," she told him, "I'm not your flavour."

"I'm all for trying new things."

"I'm not," Alex said truthfully and turned away from his wicked grin.

But he wasn't finished. "Can I offer you a lift home?"

"I have a ride, thank you. Cass and Caro are staying at Viv's house, just up the street." She hurried out into the hall where guests were saying goodnight to the couple. They would spend the night in their home and depart for a short honeymoon in the morning, Eleuthera having tactfully checked herself and the out-of-town guests into a hotel to give them privacy.

Alex hugged the newlyweds warmly and went to find her coat, only to have it placed around her shoulders by JJ. She muttered a stiff "Thanks" and searched for the twins. Desperately, she tried to pretend Mr. Dimples wasn't right on her heels.

"We've decided to go to the hotel for a little post-party party. Everyone's invited," Caro told her. "Or we can drop you off first if you're tired."

"I am tired," Alex said, unable to hide a yawn, "but I'll get a cab."

"Nonsense," interjected the aggravating man behind her. "I can drop you." He slipped an arm around her and grinned affably. "I know the way."

That was it. She was boxed in. Smiling as brightly as she could, she let him lead her off.

"I don't know what it is about me that offends you," he

groused as he fired up the sporty jeep. "I mean, an invitation to supper or a movie hardly sounds like an insult."

Alex kept her attention on the passing scenery.

"I'm an easy-going guy. I have all my own hair and teeth." He tapped his fingers impatiently on the wheel. "I'm self-supporting . . . kind to animals."

There was a loose thread on her pants. She plucked it off.

"I give to local charities and international child relief on a regular basis."

She coughed.

"My socks match. Usually. Did I say that already?"

"What does it stand for?" she asked curiously.

Thrown at the change of subject, he looked askance. "What?"

"Your initials. Is it John Jacob or Julian Joseph or —"

"It's J-A-Y J-A-Y," he spelled.

"You're lying."

Blushing, he growled, "My mother had a twisted sense of humor. Let it go."

Flicking him a glance, she pointed out, "You're going the wrong way."

"No, I'm just taking a more relaxing route." There was a full minute of silence. "How about we go to a movie sometime?"

"I can't."

"Why not?"

"Too many things to do. Responsibilities. Some of us do have them."

"I'm responsible," he replied, sounding aggrieved.

"Then you'll understand if I have to say no, thank you."

"What responsibilities can one have that don't allow for a night out every now and then?"

"How about elderly parents and two rambunctious sons who are extremely hard to find sitters for?" *Not to mention expensive to find sitters for.*

JJ's head whipped around at that. "You have kids?"

"The light is red," she shouted.

He slammed on the brakes, which gave them both a good jolt.

"Sorry," he said. Oddly disappointed at the notion of his being put off by the idea of children, Alex was surprised when he suggested a few minutes later, "I like kids. We could take them to a movie."

"Listen," she stated perversely, "I'm just not in a position right now to be dating, let alone to give Hank and Billy ideas about someone who won't stick around long."

"How can you say I won't stick around? You don't even know me," he protested in a rising voice.

"Have you ever sustained any semblance of a meaningful relationship with a member of the opposite sex?" she demanded.

"I could learn."

"Get your education elsewhere, Vanzant. I have too much going on." Alex spared him one hard look, trying not to let his shuttered expression tug on her emotions. She was being rather harsh, she conceded, but she was smart enough to recognize that she only presented a challenge to him and she dared not start thinking otherwise.

The rest of the ride was in silence, and she was in the midst of composing an apology when he pulled into her parents' driveway.

"I'm sor—"

"Forget it," he said, cutting her off. "I should have taken no for an answer the first time." Smiling a little sadly, he capitulated, "You're right, anyway. I *am* a bad risk. I'll wait until you're inside before I leave."

Knowing when to let well enough alone, Alex got out and tiredly trudged up the walk to the tiny white house and let herself in. The fading sound of the jeep seemed very lonely as she leaned against the closed door.

Later, after she'd checked on her sleeping boys and changed into her old pajamas, she paused before the full-length mirror in the hall. Scrutinizing her body from every angle, she told herself it was for the best that she never see JJ again. He was having a laugh at her expense, that was all.

The only thing that still made her resemble the old Alex was her lustrous, curling black hair. She fingered the strands reaching just past her thin shoulders and added her breasts to the short list. They, by some miracle, were still full and proud. Now if only the rest of her body—hell, her *life*—would catch up, she'd be happy.

She lay on her narrow bed in the dark and wondered what JJ had meant when he'd told her he was a bad risk. She sensed that something solitary and troubling lurked beneath those words, their meaning attached to a much deeper experience than skirt-chasing.

It was not her concern, she reminded herself. It mattered nothing if she'd experienced a twinge of remorse after turning him down so coldly. She'd likely only run into him occasionally through Viv and Jonas—and not then if she could avoid it.

Chapter Two

"What do you mean when you say you can't take notes *shorthand?*" JJ demanded of the woman standing in front of his desk. "You are a qualified administrative assistant, are you not?" The dangerously low tone he was using should have been a hint that he was not in the greatest of moods. The tense set of shoulders stretching the crisp white cotton of his shirt was another clue. "I interviewed you four days ago, at which time you assured me you were fully capable of performing the tasks expected of a secretary. I even saw an authentic certificate."

"I passed the course without having to take shorthand, sir," the twenty-something blonde with the biggest hair and matching chest he'd ever seen informed him as she smacked her gum without much enthusiasm. "The instructor said it was obsolete, anyway, and that my accommodating personality would make up for it." She beamed at him through lips painted blood-red and toyed with the buttons on her blouse, *accidentally* popping one open.

Closing his eyes, JJ inhaled through gritted teeth and braced both hands on his desk. "Your instructor said that?"

"Yup. He was very complimentary."

"*He?*"

"Uh-huh." Another button followed the first.

"*He was wrong! Out!*" His roar could undoubtedly be heard throughout the offices of his firm and possibly several on the upper and lower floors of the building it was in.

"But I'm a very good receptionist," Brandy protested,

clearly not bright enough to get going while the going was good.

He strode to the door and flung it wide. "Nance!" he bellowed. "Get this person out of my sight!"

The forty-two-year-old skip-tracer ambled over to his office and stuck her head inside. "Let's go, Ms. Gill. If you're lucky, the agency won't hear of this soon."

The no-nonsense tone galvanized Brandy into action, and she fled without another suggestive word.

"How do you do that?" JJ wondered aloud.

Nance pushed her wire-rimmed spectacles farther up her nose. "Three kids and a husband so soft he's virtually redundant in the discipline department. What's your problem? I thought you'd hire that one. The first two left in tears, for cryin' out loud."

"I would have given the girl the job if she took shorthand and kept her clothes on."

"Ah, boss," she lamented, following him back inside, "it's those eyes. She probably thought you were saying no but you really meant yes."

He grunted and paced the large office.

"I've never known you to be in such a rotten mood. Jerry and Spike are even looking both ways before leaving their rat holes." Nance watched him walk the length of the room. "It's a woman."

"Have you ever seen me distracted by a woman?" he scoffed.

"So, it's a special woman. I knew it'd happen one day."

Nance Green had been in the same foster home as JJ for a year and had volunteered herself as his big sister and champion since his tenth birthday. They'd managed to keep in touch sporadically over the years, and she'd been the first person he'd thought to hire when he'd gone into business on his own six years ago. She had a knack for tracking down bail-jumpers and she kept him on his toes.

"You knew what would happen?"

"Don't play dense, it doesn't work with me. You met a woman, and she's giving you the fits."

"What is it with you married people?" he asked her. "You lot are not content unless everyone around you is chained to a ball, too."

"Hmph," she crabbily interrupted, "you're extremely moody for a so-called happy bachelor. The ball and chain does have its advantages, you know." Studying a fingernail closely, she resumed, "I get free massages, breakfast in bed once a week, and some very creative physical activity —"

"Stop!" He covered his ears. "Forget I brought it up."

"Yeah, you did bring it up." She laughed.

JJ stopped in front of the bay window and stared out across downtown St. John's.

Sunlight glinted off the moving traffic below, and pedestrians hurried along on the snow-dusted sidewalks. The bustle had his aching head throbbing harder, reminding him he'd had three nights of tossing and turning simply because he couldn't stand the fact that Alex didn't want his company. Or rather, she did but wouldn't admit to it.

Why he cared so much for a woman he barely knew was a mystery. Perhaps it was those big, sad eyes, or that luscious mouth, or the way her slim body had molded to his while they'd danced. It hadn't been just dancing he'd dreamed of doing with her in those few hours he'd managed to drift off in the night.

"I have to go out for a bit, Nance. That appointment with the insurance guy on Duckworth can't wait. If anyone else shows up about the job —"

"I'll grill them myself. You can count on me." She eyed him with concern. "I'm a good listener, too."

JJ tried a smile. "I know. Maybe later." He pulled on his

jacket and overcoat, sweeping up his briefcase on the way out the door. He was thankful to escape the tedious round of second interviews.

On the elevator ride down to the lobby, he contemplated pumping Jonas for information on Alex. He should be back from his abbreviated honeymoon by that evening. A casual call to see how his trip went wouldn't seem amiss. But that was to think about later, when he didn't have clients to meet and a secretary to find.

Chin in hand, Alex stared morosely at the pitiful balance on her bank statement. *Fifteen dollars and fifty-six cents.*

How was she supposed to put food on the table, help her parents pay the bills, and buy the boys' Christmas presents with fifteen dollars and fifty-six cents?

The pressure building in her head all morning increased, a persistent migraine blurring her vision as she wearily changed the website on the old laptop to hunt through the day's want ads in the local paper.

Circling an advertisement for waitress positions at a nightclub, she reluctantly conceded that sticking to the area of secretary-slash-administrative assistant had gotten her nowhere. The few interviews she'd gotten had been disasters. One woman had asked if she spoke German—that was a requirement she'd left out of the ad. Two balding men had enquired whether or not she objected to working weekends at a local hotel—but not doing secretarial work, if their leers were interpreted correctly.

Alex was the first to admit that her credentials were measly. The certificate she'd obtained after completing a rudimentary course in typing and shorthand was not highly regarded, the school having gone bankrupt upon her graduation.

The credits she'd worked so hard for in university when she'd dreamed of becoming a teacher were not applicable to office jobs and, therefore, disregarded. One more semester was all it would have taken to get her degree. One more semester. She sighed, wondering for the umpteenth time why she'd let Darryl convince her to drop out and stay at home before Hank had even been born.

"You don't need to work, Al," he'd said confidently, "when I'll be making more than enough to support a family."

So, smitten and naive, she'd given up on her own career and helped her husband with his. She'd typed up his papers and briefs, made sure he was properly dressed to impress his fellow accountants, played the happy homemaker, and never objected to having too much time on her hands.

By the time Hank was a year old and she'd become pregnant with Billy, things had unraveled.

One day, Alex had gone shopping for new clothes for Hank as he'd outgrown most of what he'd had. She'd picked up several small t-shirts and pants and wheeled them up to the cash register. She'd given the cashier a credit card only to have the woman hand it back while snootily informing her that it would not be accepted. Alex had fished out another card and then another, but they had all been canceled. Flushed with embarrassment, for about twenty customers had been close enough to witness her humiliation, she'd been forced to leave the items on the counter.

She'd been so sure that it was all a big mistake when she'd told Darryl about the credit cards, so certain that he'd make a phone call and everything would be straightened out. What a fool she'd been.

Her husband had shrugged and said the cards were a nuisance anyway and they'd been paying too much interest. In reality, he'd not only borrowed on them for gambling trips she hadn't known he was taking, but he'd drained the joint bank accounts as well. He'd singlehandedly put them in hock up to the eyeballs playing poker and blackjack in another province when she'd believed he was attending seminars and meeting with clients.

As angry and disillusioned as Alex had been, she'd vowed they could handle it together and had enrolled in a six-week secretarial course and went to work. Darryl had agreed that with the combined income they could pay off his debts fairly quickly. He'd sworn to give up gambling for good. He hadn't.

The clincher for Alex had come when she'd discovered her husband had not only been throwing away money around the casinos, but that he'd been spending it on a mistress. That had killed what little love and respect for Darryl she'd managed to hold on to. She'd packed her bags and taken the boys to her parents' house and filed for divorce.

Obligation had made her go back, however, when he'd been diagnosed with a terminal illness. He'd needed her, and she couldn't refuse.

For the next two years, Darryl had blamed her for everything from his infidelity to his unfortunate medical condition. It had been Alex's fault that he'd sought the company of another woman—someone much more attractive and accommodating—and if he hadn't been so stressed out by her leaving him, he would never have gotten sick. Logically, she knew the last accusation was ridiculous. Emotionally, the first charge found its intended target, and she'd thought she was lacking sexually. She hadn't been angry for that at first. In fact, she'd attributed his cruel behavior to his illness and the drugs he was forced to take to relieve his discomfort. By the time he'd passed, Darryl had chipped away at her self-esteem so that only a trace of it remained.

Head in her hands now, Alex didn't notice her mother entering the kitchen until she spoke.

"Anything new?" Lorna Eldrich asked as she moved around the table. In her late fifties, the woman looked twenty years older — the strain of Alex's situation had taken its toll on everyone. Her gray hair was twisted into a bun, her dress faded and worn from washing.

Guilt swamped her as she dully replied, "Not much."

"You know what you need." Lorna carefully placed a teacup in a saucer. "You need a—"

"Mom," Alex groaned, dreading the familiar lecture.

"—man."

There it was. Out again.

"A man is what got me into this mess in the first place."

"But, darling, you can't do it all on your own." A throwback to another era, her mother was a firm believer in the barefoot and pregnant scenario. A man's job was to provide a roof overhead, and a woman's was to provide everything else for the man and his children.

"I let someone hold the purse strings before, and look what it got me. Ignorance is not necessarily bliss." Tiredly, she scrubbed her hands down her face. The migraine was not going away. "I can't believe you keep trying to persuade me to get a man."

Lorna clucked. "Even on a secretary's income you can't make enough to properly care for the kids. I still think you should talk to the Mannings."

"No way," Alex wearily objected. Darryl's parents had kept their distance from their grandchildren, showing next to no interest in them save the obligatory birthday card. They had offered no monetary assistance, and she was loath to subject the boys to their snobby attitudes.

"Elizabeth and Gerard have money, Alex."

"They don't have as much as they'd like people to think. Besides, they still believe I trapped Darryl into marriage."

This was laughable, considering it had been his idea. To his parents, however, she hadn't been good enough for their only son. They'd pinned their hopes on his sister having kids someday on whom they could shower affection, even if they did live in Europe.

Alex went to take a painkiller and returned to the tiny kitchen to find her mother had settled down at the table for the long version of her argument.

"I do not need a man to take care of me."

"Alex, you're too pale, too thin, too exhausted all the time. You have no energy for the children and no money for food and clothes, let alone Christmas gifts." Although her tone had gentled, there was still an underlying thread of steel accompanying her words.

"I'm sorry, Mom. I know this is hard on you and Dad, but I'm sure something good will happen soon."

"It's been months since you brought in a paycheck, and public aid is meager at best. I'm worried about you, Alex." Tears glistened in the older woman's eyes as she looked at her only child.

A sting itched behind her lids. Alex patted a work-roughened hand. "I'll find something. I have to post these résumés." She shrugged into her old woolen parka and left the house, despondently thinking that her parents shouldn't have to fret over their adult daughter.

The chilly November air nipped at her bare hands but seemed to ease her headache a little on her walk to the end of the street. After she'd shoved the mail through the flap in the receptacle, she turned back toward home. Passing Viv Wilder-Mackenzie's brick house had her thinking fleetingly of a certain PI, and she let his image linger. It was the first time that day she forgot to worry about anything.

One ring . . . two rings . . . three rings.

JJ bounced a pencil on his blotter irritably as he waited to connect with someone at the Mackenzie estate.

The day had gone downhill since the mini-fiasco with Brandy. The client he was supposed to meet hadn't shown up, he'd dented his beloved jeep in a parking garage along with some guy's sports car, the weather had turned from a light snow forecast to near whiteout conditions, and just as he'd made it back to the relative calm of his building without another incident or injury, the elevator had stalled with him in it, creating a mild panic attack.

He hated elevators and any small enclosed space. It reminded him of Mrs. Botnik's closet and the time he'd spent there. Usually, he managed to keep his head in a lift for as long as it took to travel from one floor to another, probably because he knew that sooner or later the door would open. Unless the power failed. Which was exactly what could happen in a blizzard.

"Mackenzie residence," a voice that JJ recognized as that of the longtime housekeeper said in his ear.

"Ms—or should I say *Mrs.* Hunt, now?" he silkily enquired.

Dottie Long had finally given in to her employer's brother, Michael Hunt, and they'd eloped just weeks before his nephew had tied the knot.

"You call me Dottie, you young scamp, like you always have."

Grinning, he couldn't resist asking, "How's married life? Are you tired of the old sod yet?"

"Never you mind. That old sod's still got twice as much get-up-and-go as you'll ever have."

JJ laughed. "Naughty woman."

She shot back, "Nothing wrong with it. And if you're looking for that redheaded fiend, he's upstairs with his wife, and I'll not be disturbing him."

"Ah, so they're back from parts unknown and won't answer their cells."

"Parts unknown—hah! She dragged him back to that Godforsaken hut again." The *Godforsaken hut* was a fully equipped, more than comfortable family lodge. It had all the amenities of home and a romantic atmosphere. Jonas had bragged that Viv got them both *stranded* there and seduced him. "Oh, here he comes now. Take care."

JJ barely had a chance to respond to her abrupt departure when Jonas came on the line. He pictured the big man reclining at his desk in the den, feet up, phone tucked under his chin.

"Trust you to call a man on his first day back from honeymooning, Vanzant." A yawn followed the grumbled remark.

"Plum tuckered you out, did she?"

Jonas chuckled slyly. "Viv is the one still napping, not me."

"As long as you're not in danger of relapsing," JJ said dryly, reminding his friend of the recent gunshot that had almost ended his life. Viv had been stalked by an unbalanced woman, and Jonas had taken a bullet while trying to protect her. Cringing at the memory of one of his closet pals lying unconscious in an intensive care unit, he beat it down resolutely and asked, "How's the chest?"

"Perfect. All healed. My wife is a gentle woman."

"She feels indebted to you for saving her life."

"Ain't gratitude grand?" the redhead chortled, knowing full well that his new bride adored him. "Why are you calling anyway?"

JJ sobered up rather quickly and pondered how to best go about his task. "Well, I was wondering if you could . . . ah . . . tell me a bit about . . ."

"Alex Manning?"

Shock pushed the air from his lungs. "Yes, but how did you know I'd be asking?"

Jonas practically snickered. "I've bet good money on you snooping around for information on her."

"With who? Viv?"

"Noooooo. Steven."

JJ huffed. "I am scandalized. That you would bet that I, pure soul that I am—"

A strange noise interrupted his disclaimer.

"—would lust after . . . did you just *snort*?"

"You'll have to ask Viv about this. I've only met Alex a few times." A female voice spoke in the background. "It's JJ, darling."

"Yuck, man. *Darling*? You've lost it."

"Careful," Viv warned as she took the phone, "I know where you work. What's this about my friend?"

He cleared his throat awkwardly. "I was hoping you could tell me a little about her."

A moment passed, then another. "And this would be personal?"

"Well, hell, Viv, I'm not investigating her or anything. I'd just like to know how to reach her."

"You want her phone number? I don't know that she'd thank me for giving it to you."

Laughter tinged her words, but they hit a sore spot with JJ.

"Jeez, I only asked her out, I swear. Am I that awful?"

A sigh came across the line. "It isn't you," Viv said gently.

"Why do I get the feeling that you're not about to tell me what *it* is?" He shoved a hand through his hair in frustration.

"It's Alex's business and very personal. I'm sorry."

"How's a guy supposed to wangle a date out of a woman

that difficult?"

"Oh," Viv's tone grew stern, "hear me now, JJ. She's been through a lot these last few years and she doesn't need someone jumping in who only wants to play with her emotions, understand? Don't you go bothering Alex unless you're serious, or you'll have me to answer to."

"I do believe Mackenzie's protective streak is rubbing off."

"I mean it!"

JJ let out a long breath and pinched the bridge of his nose. "I hear you."

"So, are you serious?" demanded Viv.

"I'll think on it," he assured her, sincere. He'd been evaluating the unfamiliar depth of his feelings for days.

"You'd better. Now that I've ruined your mood, is there anything I can do to make up for it?"

He actually laughed at that. "My mood was ruined when I got up this morning." He proceeded to sketch out his rotten day.

"Poor JJ. I might be able to help in your search for a new employee," she imparted. "If only I'd known sooner, I could have saved you some trouble—and misery."

The cryptic comment perked him up. "You've been stashing a typist. Please tell me you've been hiding a multi-talented office worker. I want a name."

"I'll send her to you if she hasn't hooked in to a job yet."

"You're being very mysterious, Mrs. Mackenzie. Can I trust you?"

She cackled, sounding mean. "Do you have a choice?"

"Does Hubby know what a wicked, wicked woman you are?"

"Believe me, he doesn't complain."

After exchanging a few more words with Jonas, JJ hung up and swiveled his chair toward the window. The snowfall had dwindled to a light flurry in the darkened sky, and lights from other buildings twinkled like stars, some going out as people left work for home.

The thought of an evening alone in his expensively sterile apartment held absolutely no appeal. He closed his eyes and tried to picture what his living room would be like with a few kids rolling around on the thick carpet, but somehow the image of little bodies romping gaily over the chrome and glass decor didn't jibe.

The incongruous vision in his head faded, and he looked to the window once again, watching the slow descent of a solitary snowflake as it drifted by.

Alex would have a warm home. The errant thought startled him for a second. Perhaps it was not simply physical attraction that drew him to her. Maybe it was just that his first glimpse of her at home in Viv's kitchen had done something to trigger a long-buried yearning for a *normal* family. Could it be that she reminded him of what he'd longed for since childhood but had accepted was unattainable?

JJ chuckled without humour. Whatever it was that made him react to Alex on a shockingly basic level had nothing to do with childhood dreams. Every dream he'd had involving her had been very *adult*.

Rousing his exhausted body, he gathered up his coat and briefcase and locked the office. As he trudged wearily to the bank of elevators, he contemplated the allure of a TV dinner over takeout and resigned himself to yet another quiet evening alone.

CHAPTER THREE

"You're glowing." Alex took in the flushed cheeks and brilliant green eyes of the woman on her doorstep.

Viv's blonde hair whipped about her, and she came inside, stomping the snow from her boots. "It's freezing out there." Tugging off her gloves, she plopped down at the kitchen table and grinned at Alex.

"I don't think it's the sub-zero temperature that's responsible for the spark in your eye." Alex poured coffee for them both and sat across from her. "I didn't expect you to be out and about so soon, Mrs. Mackenzie."

Viv rolled her eyes and wrapped grateful hands around the mug. "I wish everyone would stop the *Mrs.* stuff. I feel old. And I probably wouldn't have bothered if I wasn't struck with the urge to see my cuties. Where are the boys?"

"Playing with the blocks Auntie Viv gave them," Alex drolly replied.

"Ah, future engineers. I like to know I've inspired the younger generation." Plucking at her sweater sleeve, she asked, "How's the job hunt going?"

Alex groaned. "I'm drowning."

"I may have a lifeline. If you can stand it, that is."

"Right now, I'll take anything if it means a decent paycheck. Did you hear of something?" Hope drove the fatigue from Alex's body as she stared at her best friend.

"I did." Viv drew circles on the linen tablecloth with the handle of her spoon. "But you may not be comfortable with it."

"Spit it out."

"JJ needs a secretary, like yesterday." Viv sipped her coffee and waited.

Poetic justice was the phrase that immediately sprang to mind for Alex. She didn't realize she'd spoken it aloud until Viv laughed.

Wiping a merry tear from her eye, she said, "Come on, JJ isn't so bad."

"Not *bad* exactly, just a tad lecherous and too damn charming for his own good." And for her own if she were honest. "But I can handle him." The statement sounded ten times more confident than she felt. "I can," she insisted when Viv laughed again.

"You should see your face. If those brown eyes get any rounder with sincerity, they might pop out."

"So what if he's asked me to dinner? I'm sure he's capable of a little professionalism," Alex claimed optimistically.

Sober now, her friend told her, "He's a good guy and he's desperate to get the position filled. Apparently, his secretary went on maternity leave and then decided to stay home with the baby. He swears his files are a wreck."

Alex figured JJ Vanzant was a wreck all his own. "How long has she been gone?"

"Weeks. I only found out when he called to pump Jonas about you. Don't worry," she said, raising a hand, "neither of us gave him any details about your personal situation. I didn't tell him were looking for work either, so it isn't some romantic ploy on his part."

Grateful for the discretion, Alex squeezed Viv's arm. She didn't need to tell Viv that what kept her going most days were Hank, Billy, and a smidgeon of pride and self-respect which she clung to with both hands.

"I can drop off a résumé in the morning."

"I think you should take the initiative and march right into his office," was Viv's staunch suggestion. "Oh, here's the address."

Alex took the proffered slip of paper and muttered, wry, "Attempting to march anywhere at my height doesn't exactly come off the way it's intended." Her ill-fitting wardrobe was not too impressive either, she reminded herself grimly. The newest outfits she had were way too loose on her skinny frame, but they'd have to do.

Two black-haired whirlwinds chose that moment to storm the kitchen and jump on Viv's lap. Hank and Billy yelled and cheered as they almost strangled her in an exuberant embrace and raced back to the living room, leaving her breathless with giggles.

"I love them. I can't wait to have some of my own."

"Time for bed, you two," Alex shouted after them. "Maybe you should cherish this time with your husband before expanding the family," she said, good-natured.

"I fully intend to. Well," Viv glanced at her watch, "I have to get going. I wanted to stop in at my house and make sure Cass and Caro haven't demolished the place. Did I tell you they're thinking about buying it and staying here?" She pulled on her coat and chatted while Alex walked her out, giving her a warm hug before stepping back into the cold.

"Ah, just one thing, Viv," Alex stalled her by saying, "and I don't mean to sound suspicious." She nibbled her lip and floundered for the right words, hoping not to come off as being prudish or snippy.

"What's that?"

"Well, I know Jonas and JJ are good friends and everything . . ."

"Hmm?" Viv's eyebrow rose, and her eyes danced.

"I really have no intention of going out with him," In an abrupt manner, she said, "I mean, if you and Jonas were trying —"

"Oh Lord! Matchmaking is not on our agenda, honey. However," continued the newlywed, "if something were to click between the two of you as you took dictation . . ."

"Nothing would click," Alex vowed, "except the keys of the computer afterward."

Smiling, Viv winked and closed the door.

JJ slapped the last file on the glass-topped coffee table and rubbed a hand over his eyes. His shoulders ached, and he was bone-deep tired, the frustrations of the day taxing him no end.

The blinking light on his phone beckoned, and he leaned over to punch a button. Rolling his head to one side and then the other to relieve the stiffness in his neck, he listened with half an ear as his messages played back—a few from select clients that he'd given his private number to, one from Steven Kincaid inviting him out for a beer on the weekend, and one from a woman he'd dated almost a year ago who thought she might like to renew their acquaintance. He vaguely recalled Veronica—her disembodied voice was slightly nasal and a bit grating.

Had he really gone out with someone who sounded that annoying? Yes, he reminisced ruefully, he had. While he'd been very circumspect in his sex life, he hadn't been too selective when it came to a woman's personality—probably because he spent very little time with anyone he dated outside the bedroom. He'd been shallow in that regard simply because he hadn't wanted to form any relationships that couldn't be considered casual. That made it easier on both parties when it came time to move on. He couldn't honestly say that he'd even developed a fondness for any particular woman who'd interested him sexually.

Until that stubborn Manning vixen with the smart mouth

had cast her soulful brown eyes his way.

JJ may have been stymied by Viv's reluctance to spill the beans about her friend's personal life, but his firm was one of the best — if not *the* best — in St. John's. If he couldn't satisfy his itch to know more about her the easy way, he'd just go another route. He could have all the information he wanted in less than twenty-four hours and no more dealing with tight-lipped friends to get it.

The phone rang, and he stretched an arm tiredly to answer. "Vanzant."

"How personal a greeting, how warm and inviting —"

"Hello, Viv."

She sighed gustily. "I hope you're more congenial to your new admin assistant."

"If she works out, I'll send you flowers."

"Oh, I'm pretty certain she'll meet your qualifications. She's got experience, she's calm and collected in a pinch, tough but agreeable, and she's a sweetheart."

"I'll believe it when I see it. An honest-to-goodness secretary," he marveled. "I may be forced to lure you away from the redhead to show my appreciation."

"Don't bother. I can't be lured."

"I figured."

Viv laughed and hung up on him.

Alex was nervous. The tight ball in the pit of her stomach clenched anew as she scanned the board in the buzzing lobby. *Fifth Floor . . . Niagra Designs . . . Barbour Investments . . . Vanzant & Co.*

Drawing a deep breath, she headed purposefully toward the elevators. She squeezed into a crowded car and pressed up against the wall, quickly surveying the other occupants. By the look of the expensively tailored suits worn by both men and women, the building that housed JJ's offices was very prestigious. Only one or two others were clothed in the same style as she, ironed linen slacks off the rack and button-down blouses. Her raglan was too thin for early December, but it was the newest coat she had. Her low-heeled pumps had offered little protection from the cold while she'd waited for the bus to take her here, so the snow had dampened her tiny feet.

A shiver raced up her spine as she watched the lit numbers climb until the car stopped on the fifth level. She followed the signs directing her to Vanzant & Co., her steps faltering momentarily when she realized the space accommodating it took up over half the floor. Obviously, JJ had done well in his field.

Alex stopped in front of the double doors to compose herself, mentally reviewing what she knew about the company. Although the basis of the operation was primarily investigation, JJ had expanded over the years to include a highly regarded security division that offered state-of-the-art systems to large corporations. The systems in question were customized to meet the precise needs of every client.

The company had grown to over fifty people, mostly investigators and technicians, and a small but efficient administrative staff.

She looked at her watch for the thousandth time that morning. Ten minutes still remained before her appointment with JJ. She'd called around nine, and a pleasant-voiced person had advised her to come at ten with résumé and any pertinent certificates. The scramble through her closet for her beige pants and matching top had been hectic, for she hadn't expected to get an interview so soon. *He must be desperate!*

Five minutes.

Although Alex had attributed her queasy stomach to the fact that she badly needed this job and therefore couldn't afford for anything to go wrong, she was aware that her prospective employer was an even bigger source of anxiety.

Working with a near-perfect specimen of masculinity who happened to be loaded with charisma and good looks wouldn't have normally been a problem. That it was JJ Vanzant who made her want to smile when she had precious little to smile about and think naughty thoughts she had no business thinking, now *that* was a conundrum. But she was confident that they could keep their dealings with each other professional — almost.

Thirty seconds.

Besides, he'd never have to know how he affected her. It was a useless attraction she felt — Mr. Dimples was out of her realm.

Just as she squared her shoulders and reached for the door handle, the oak panel was flung wide, and the most garishly dressed man she'd ever seen yanked her inside.

Slamming the door behind her, he said, "I'm Jerry. Tell me you're Alexandra." His gray hair was bound by a rubber band, and his shirt was spattered with a blinding floral print that no man ought to be caught dead wearing. His jeans were faded through at the knees, the seams about to separate and drop right off his spare frame. The blazer he sported had one black sleeve, one red, and the vest was a splotchy mixture of both. Neon yellow tennis shoes completed the frightening ensemble.

Speechless, she just stared into Jerry's hazel eyes.

"Well?" he shot forth again in a voice as startling as his outfit.

"Y-yes, I'm Alex Manning." She barely got the words out when he literally picked her up and carried her past several gaping people and down a hallway.

Jerry deposited her in what appeared to be the inner sanctum, bellowed, "Nance!" and shut the door.

Stunned to hear the lock turning, Alex teetered unsteadily

on her feet and dropped her portfolio.

"You'll have to ignore him," someone instructed from behind her. "Jerry is the resident genius and overall freak. *Nice to meet you* is not in his vocabulary. I'm Nancy Green—Nance." The forty-something woman smiled and offered her hand. Intelligent green eyes twinkled from behind her glasses as she prodded, "I guess you're Alex."

Still dazed, she managed to fumble a handshake and murmur, "How do you do?"

Nance indicated she take a seat and pulled a pencil from her curly brown hair. "The rest of us aren't nearly as warped as Jerry, believe me."

"He was a little . . . uh . . ."

"Abnormal." It was a definitive statement.

"This is a nice office." Alex crossed her legs and surveyed the outer room. Three doors led off the reception area, one of them with JJ's name on it. The large windows allowing a breathtaking view of downtown St. John's and the waterfront created a spacious, airy atmosphere. The furniture was modern and sleek, the tables topped with glass. A large desk sat to the left with a pile of crammed folders, a phone, and a high-tech computer system crowding the top of it. File cabinets lined the walls on the right.

"You're hired." Nance closed the brief portfolio Alex hadn't noticed she'd even opened and beamed at her.

"Just like that?" Surprise mingled with relief, and she tried to close her mouth. "Don't I have to see Mr. Vanzant?"

"Oh no, he was called to an emergency earlier. Don't worry, I can see that you have tons of experience for this job."

"I can start soon?" Alex couldn't believe her luck. A sudden thought occurred, and she had to ask, "JJ didn't tell you to hire me regardless of my qualifications, did he?"

Nance studied her closely. "Actually, he was gone when you called. I guess you were the one referred by a friend of his?" She paused when Alex nodded. "Hmm. He said he didn't know your name—I just assumed that I had the right one when I spoke to you. It was Viv Mackenzie who sent you to us, right?"

"Yes."

"Oh good. I thought I mighta goofed." Nance chuckled. "As for your previous question, the bottom line is this . . . work is piling up, the boss is unusually tense, and we'd all like to get dug out of this mess," she waved a hand toward the desk, "before Christmas. Now, you can type proficiently, take shorthand, handle the software and the phone. *So, you're hired!*"

An hour later, Alex was knee-deep in paperwork and attempting to make sense of an impossibly twisted filing system. The phone trilled every two minutes. An irate man who'd identified himself as Spike kept buzzing and communicating through a series of grunts that he needed to see the boss as soon as he materialized. The computers went offline for twenty minutes, thus causing a string of people she assumed were her new coworkers to demand if she knew what was wrong with them.

All in all, it was a chaotic morning.

Alex gave up trying to neaten her French braid and just let the wispy thing alone. After tucking her blouse back into the waistband of her too-loose slacks for the third time, she glanced up to find that she was being watched.

JJ had apparently returned from his emergency and now stood immobile just inside the office door, a strange expression on his face.

The pencil clenched between Alex's teeth fell to the desk blotter. Closing her mouth—for it seemed to have been open since the moment she'd gotten pulled across the threshold— she straightened and said, most politely, "Hello, Mr. Vanzant."

JJ blinked. Twice. After the second time, she was still there.

Fuzzily, he wondered if a higher power had decided to play a cosmic joke and cause him to hallucinate. Was the frazzled vision before him just a figment of his imagination, a product of his thwarted libido? Or was she really standing there expectantly, waiting for his stupid mouth to work as her cheeks flushed wildly?

He approached her slowly, half afraid she'd disappear. "I didn't know you did administrative work. I'm assuming that's why you're here and not because you changed your mind about a movie and couldn't resist tracking me down?"

Alex ran a hand over her braid in what he took to be a nervous gesture. "You assume correctly. Nance told me to go ahead and get started."

He examined the desk through narrowed eyes. "You seem to have made a dent in the Heap of Hell."

"Yes," she replied, wringing her small hands. "Although your filing system is a little confusing."

"It doesn't confuse me."

"Seems you're the only one."

JJ smiled broadly. "So they tell me."

"If you like, I could —"

"No." No one, absolutely *no one* arranged his files. "I like the office just the way it is now."

Alex passed him a handful of messages, clearly trying her best to avoid touching him. "Spike keeps buzzing every fifteen minutes, and Nance would like a word when you're free."

He shuffled the slips of paper absently as he continued to study her. Her black hair was fastened securely, but several strands feathered her forehead and cheeks endearingly. She wore no makeup except a touch of gloss on her sweet mouth.

"You're staring." She folded her arms and glared at him. "If my working here is going to be a problem, I'd like to know now."

Clearing his throat, he lied, "I can't see any reason why you shouldn't work here." How the devil was he supposed to get anything done with her not twenty feet from his own desk? "If Nance thinks you're qualified, then I don't foresee any problem. Did she go over the details of your salary and such?"

"Ah, no."

"Well, it's almost time for lunch. I'll pop in on Nance and see what Spike wants, then we'll go down to the cafeteria. I want to give you a rundown of everything we do here, as well." JJ was surprised at his business-like tone, considering he'd grown shockingly aroused beneath his overcoat. No woman had ever made him react that way just by doing . . . *nothing*.

He was definitely going to have to find Alex another job. A job where she didn't distract the boss—a female boss if he could find one. This was a task he could only entrust to Nance. Pivoting abruptly, he stalked toward her office and went in without knocking.

Nance waved him to a chair and continued to argue with a parolee's girlfriend over his whereabouts, trying to coax a tidbit of information out of her. Finally, she tossed the phone back in the cradle in disgust.

"Having a bad day, are we?" JJ enquired.

"Don't ask. Everything all right at Mervin's?"

"Yeah. Some green security guard tripped the alarm by accident. No harm done." He slouched in a wing chair and eyed his friend. "I need a favour."

"Uh-oh. Sounds ominous." Nance leaned her elbows on the desk and gave him her full attention.

No matter what, JJ had always been able to count on her.

"It's about the new employee."

"Alex? She's only been here a couple of hours, and already you have a complaint?" She frowned momentarily, but then her expression cleared. "That's the one?" she asked, incredulous.

"The one what?"

"The woman who had you looking meaner than a grizzly yesterday. Well, I'll be darned. You've actually gone and got yourself interested in a female with intelligence and personality."

JJ sat up. "Don't get excited. She doesn't like me very well."

Nance laughed uproariously and clapped. "Wow! This must be a new experience for you. So, what's the favour? You want me to sing your praises, tout your good deeds?"

"No, I want you to discreetly find her a job somewhere else."

"Wouldn't it help your cause if she stayed within close range?"

"Nance, I don't want to come off looking like some hot-around-the-belt-buckle employer trying to get it on with his secretary," he said irritably.

"Aren't you?"

"That's beside the point. I don't want her thinking I'm trying to take advantage. Alex is a proud woman, and she doesn't seem very trusting of men. If I blunder into this, I'll ruin it before it even gets going." With a grim face, he contemplated the gray winter sky over Nance's shoulder.

"Okay. I see what you're saying, but it might take a while to find a place for her." She grinned, all cheek. "I hope you can keep your hands to yourself in the meantime. If you can't,

you'll just have to fire her."

"That isn't funny," JJ admonished. "I can't fire a widow with two sons."

"Well, now I am perplexed. A thinking, breathing woman with kids," she mused. "What has gotten into you?"

"I don't know . . . and I don't know if I like it." He scowled when Nance doubled over and guffawed.

After having lunch with JJ, Alex felt as if an invisible band around her chest had broken, leaving her to breathe easily for the first time in months. The salary he quoted was higher than she'd expected, and it came with a family medical plan.

He was cordial as they sat together, his words crisp and impersonal. Alex watched the way he spoke with his hands, gesturing now and then, informing her that Vanzant & Co. provided services that ranged from skip-tracing and tailing cheating spouses to installing security systems and investigating corporate espionage.

She discovered he held a degree in communications and that he'd spent a few years in law enforcement.

It was impossible not to notice how other women in the cafeteria showed an obvious interest in him — they deliberately brushed by him in the line-up or bumped their table to say hello. He appeared not to pay any heed and continued to describe his company with growing enthusiasm.

There was one awkward moment when he startled her by asking, "By the way, do you need an advance?"

Alex shot her head up and tried to read his expression, but his attention was focused on his spoon while he stirred sugar into his coffee. Had the state of her clothing tipped him off to her dire financial situation?

"Do you normally offer new employees advances?" she stiffly probed.

"If I know them enough not to worry about them showing up for work after I've signed the check."

"And you think you know me well enough?"

He lifted his sapphire gaze and quirked an eyebrow. "Why, Alex, we were in the same wedding party just last weekend. At the very least, I can hunt you down if you take the money and run."

"True." She nearly smiled back at him. "If you don't mind . . ."

JJ shook his blond head, and the subject was dropped. The offhanded way he'd made the offer left her at ease when she went back to work.

The afternoon flew by, and she was ready to leave when Nance strolled out of her office.

"How'd you like your first day?" she asked, sticking a pencil in its familiar place behind an ear.

Alex smiled cordially. "Hectic but interesting."

"That filing system is something else, huh? The boss detests change."

"I'll work on it," she proffered in a low voice.

Nance was not the lone complainant in that area.

"He's not always that stubborn, honest. JJ is actually very adaptable in most things." The look she gave Alex said she was referring to things outside the office as well. "He's a good guy."

Alex reflected later that it was the second time in as many days that she'd been told that. The man had a list of fans. Hopefully, she could keep from adding herself to it.

CHAPTER FOUR

Alex paced the length of her employer's office in agitation. For four days she'd tried to understand why he insisted on having everything filed in clumps labelled Intelligence, Security, Personal Dossiers, et cetera. It was virtually impossible to locate anything in under fifteen minutes.

Coupled with that, JJ had reverted back to his goofball persona, which scared the hell out of her. It had been much easier to ignore him when he'd acted serious and gentlemanly than when he made jokes and waggled his eyebrows at her.

Several times during the week, she'd caught him sizing her up from a distance, and he'd made no secret of the fact that he was still interested.

Her nerves were strung tight, and she figured she may as well try to convince him to let her rearrange his chaos one last time.

"Alphabetically," she pleaded.

"Too unimaginative." His faded jeans clung lovingly to his long legs and lean hips, and his booted feet rested on the corner of his desk. His black t-shirt hugged a well-defined chest that she thought would pillow a woman's tired head perfectly. As he laced his fingers together over a flat stomach, she admired the flex of bulging biceps.

Gritting her teeth to drive away the desire she'd been fighting a daily battle with, she ground out, "Chronologically."

"Jeez, Alex, I can barely remember what year I finished high school, let alone when I followed Mrs. Hawthorne to a clandestine rendezvous with her gardener."

"I can't find anything out there, JJ, it's all one monstrous jumble."

"The last two could find stuff."

Alex stared. "The last two secretaries quit out of sheer

frustration."

"How'd you find out about that?" He scratched his head and looked a bit guilty. "I went to all that trouble making everyone think I fired them."

"It was an exercise in futility. Just like this conversation," she muttered.

Grinning, he rocked his chair slightly, the motion reminding her of a very intimate activity.

"First thing Monday, I'm putting your files in alphabetical order."

"No, you're not. I'm the boss."

"The most disorganized boss on the continent."

JJ dropped his feet to the floor and stood. "My mind works better that way." He perched on the side of the desk and snaked out an arm, surprising her by pulling her into the vee of his thighs.

"What are you doing?" she demanded breathlessly.

He rubbed her back slowly, kneading the tense muscles with his big hands. "You've been uptight all week, Alex. You're going to have to learn to relax."

A protest died on her lips when she looked into his blue eyes, and the stress of the last several days dropped away. He stroked from her shoulders to the small of her back, all the while watching her face intently.

"Good?" he murmured.

"Mmm." Without meaning to, she let her forehead rest against his. When she realized what she'd done, she told herself to straighten up, but it just felt so good . . .

"God, you're a tiny thing. I can fit my hands around your waist." His voice had lowered to a whisper even though the others had gone home for the weekend. The office was deserted except for them.

"I hafta catch a bus," she slurred a few minutes later. "Just rub that spot a bit more."

"Here?" he breathed, gently massaging between her shoulder blades.

"Mmm-hmm."

If she sighed and arched her back that way once more, JJ was going to lose it. His jeans had become a little too snug, and his hands were disobeying his brain. He knew better than to touch any part of her, but he'd convinced himself that a minute or two couldn't possibly . . .

"Mmm. Lower."

. . . hurt.

He slipped his obliging fingers beneath the waistband of her black linen skirt and found the tail of her blouse. Carefully, he worked his hands under the cotton fabric and nearly groaned when he made contact with smooth, warm skin.

Shameful, a nagging voice inside him scolded. *The woman told you she doesn't want to get involved, but here you are, manhandling her. And now she's your employee.*

She isn't objecting now, he shot back, *and I asked her out before I hired her.*

That excuses your lustful behaviour?

JJ stilled his hands. *Who the hell asked you, anyway?* He grumbled and pressed his lips to Alex's slender neck. *Just a few more kisses before she comes to her senses and goes ballistic.*

Slowly, he slid his arms around until his hands rested just below her breasts. She tipped her head back when his mouth trailed up the column of her throat, pausing to open and place a hot caress on the underside of her jaw. He raggedly whispered her name and dragged his hungry mouth across her cheek, stopping to search her face for a sign of rejection. He kept watching her as he feathered his lips over hers, but her eyes remained closed, the thick, dark lashes fanning her flushed skin.

Finally, unable to hold back any longer, JJ slanted his

mouth across hers and drank deeply from her sweet lips. Once, twice, then a third time, he pulled at their fullness before delving his tongue past them.

Later, maybe he would try to pinpoint the exact moment he lost control. It might have been when her soft breasts brushed his chest—or maybe it was when she slid a delicate hand through his hair—or that explosive second when she made a sexy sound in the back of her throat. Regardless of the cause, his composure shattered, and he kissed her like a starving man at a feast, hotly fusing his mouth to hers. He gripped her waist and ground against her, making her aware of the shocking urgency of his desire, the erotic friction driving him crazy.

In the next instant, Alex was across the room and he was nursing a stinging cheek. Shaking visibly, she fumbled to shove her blouse back inside her skirt. She looked at him as if she were mortified by her behaviour. When she spoke, he realized it was more than that.

"I'm sorry. I didn't mean to do that." Her brown eyes were huge in her pale face, and he recognized something in her expression that he'd never expected to see. Fear. She was afraid of him.

Well, hell, Vanzant, what did you expect? You almost crushed the woman while you were groping her.

JJ closed his eyes and cursed his clumsiness, berating himself for not being more careful of her. When he glanced at her again, he mustered up a grin.

"I must say, you have a deadly aim. But you're not the one who should be apologizing." He rubbed his face. "Not for kissing you, but I could have shown some finesse. I must outweigh you by a good hundred pounds."

Alex seemed surprised. "You didn't hurt me, JJ."

"Good. I'd never intentionally do that—I just got carried away." Relief sagged his shoulders. "You probably should have slapped me sooner."

"I'm not about to get fired, am I?"

He stared at her. Then, grasping the notion that she was serious, he angrily pushed away from the desk and returned to his chair. In a curt voice, he said, "I don't normally harass women in the workplace, Alex. Your job is not in jeopardy if you knock me down a notch. I didn't intend to end up pawing you, I only meant to ease some of the tension from your shoulders. I was out of line."

"I'm sorry, I didn't think before I said that." She folded her arms and solemnly continued, "It's just that I've been propositioned before, and it's made me a bit cynical, I guess."

"Would it help if I promise not to make a pass at you in the office?"

"It would be better if I'm going to work here."

JJ tried to smile reassuringly. "All right. No more kissing in the office. But if I happen to run into you anywhere else, all bets are off." When she started to protest, he shook his head. "You can deny it all you want, Alex, but you were kissing me back."

The color that rushed up her neck was immensely satisfying to him. "I've been alone a long time, and you're very attractive. Who could blame me?"

He shuffled some papers on the desk and tried not to seem particularly interested when he probed, "Do you still miss your husband?"

"Darryl?"

"Never mind," he said contrarily. "That's none of my business." And frankly, he dreaded the answer. He'd wondered over the past week if she still loved the man, if she was the type of person to only fall in love once in a lifetime. It bothered him, sometimes haunted him even, that she might not have any room left in her heart for a romantic relationship. Not that he wanted her to love him, he told himself. He'd never really believed in it, never expected it, and certainly had never heard those three little words spoken in reference to him. JJ had managed just fine without them.

"Well, I've got to get home. Hank and Billy will be driving my parents nuts by now." Alex went back to the outer office, and he followed.

"I'll give you a lift. I've made you miss your bus."

"It's no problem, another one will be by in—"she checked her watch "—two minutes." She scrambled for her coat, snatching up her purse as she shrugged it on.

"I'll have to insist, I'm afraid. It's dark, snowing, and I'll have nightmares if I don't see you safely home." He feigned a tortured expression.

"It's out of your way."

"It doesn't matter." JJ placed the back of his hand to his forehead and sighed dramatically. "However would I sleep . . ."

Alex eventually gave in, actually smiling—*smiling*—at him when he clicked his heels and grabbed a fleece-lined bomber jacket.

Traffic was lighter than usual, and he drove toward her neighbourhood. Most people had left the hub of the city by five, trying to beat the rush, heading home to their families for the weekend. It was nearly six-thirty now—he'd waylaid Alex by telling her he *absolutely* had to have a letter typed up before she left and then lifted an item from her purse while she'd been otherwise occupied. The argument over his filing system had taken even longer and then . . . well, time had ceased to exist while they'd been kissing.

"I hope I didn't keep you too late." He downshifted and coasted past stores decorated gaily for the Christmas season. The shoppers were already trudging through the snow, eager to shorten their lists as soon as possible.

"Oh, I don't mind. Mom can handle the boys for an extra

hour. I called earlier, and she was suspiciously accommodating when I said I'd be held up."

"This year must have been difficult for your family." For a second, he didn't think she'd respond, and he waited.

She seemed to be gauging the sincerity of his comment. "Money's been scarce since I lost my job." She shrugged and tossed him a semi-grin. "But now, my parents can stop worrying so much about us. They've been wonderfully supportive."

Not completely comfortable with the subject of family, he nevertheless forced himself to ask about her children. The tender expression that he glimpsed when the headlights from a passing car flooded the jeep was just reward. She seemed to soak up the artificial glow and radiate the natural version back out through her eyes while she described her boys.

Although similar in their dark-haired, blue-eyed looks, her sons were as different as night and day, she told him.

Hank was six and more serious than his brother. He was a good student in his first-grade class and fairly quiet. Even at such a young age, he exhibited the traits of a logical thinker, taking in information and seeming to sort through it meticulously before voicing an observation.

Billy, the five-year-old human hurricane, was so unlike Hank that she'd often wondered if he'd been switched at birth. He was unpredictable and sporadic in his interests, often jumping from one subject to another with endless questions.

It was clear to JJ that Alex adored her children. He listened raptly for the remainder of the ride as she related funny incidents involving them and her parents.

Just when he turned onto her street, he gave in to the urge to find out a little more about her late husband. Hoping he didn't sound just plain nosy, he enquired if Hank and Billy missed their father.

Alex exhaled slowly. "Well, they don't really remember much about Darryl. They were only three and four years old when he died." She paused, as if choosing her words carefully. "I was a stay-at-home parent, and he was always busy with work in the beginning. After he got sick, he sort of drew into himself and paid very little attention to anything, including the boys. I think he had trouble drumming up interest between the pain, the medication, and just feeling lousy." She stared out the window, clearly lost in memories.

"Dad spends time with them," she continued a minute later. "He takes them on mini fishing trips and to the occasional ball game. Mom says those are the only times he can drag himself away from the television."

JJ smiled back briefly and pulled into the driveway. He much preferred hearing about her life from her than reading through the file Spike had brought him three days ago. He hadn't spared a glance at the dossier. It felt almost like a betrayal that he'd underhandedly gone behind her back to gather information about her personal life, but he'd had Spike digging around a mere few hours before he'd discovered that she was firmly ensconced in his office. The deed had been done by then, so he'd just buried the file in his desk and ignored it.

"Thanks for bringing me home and letting me talk your ear off." She slipped out of the seat belt.

"I like hearing you talk about yourself. Do you know you have a very sexy voice?" Resting an arm on the wheel, he gave a quirky grin.

Alex rolled her eyes.

"No, really," JJ insisted. "It has a throaty, husky inflection. Very nice."

"Not to change the subject—because it is extremely flattering—but I still intend to organize your files."

"Ugh! Just like a woman to move in and start changing everything around," he joked, knowing it would get her dander up.

"How sexist!"

"And before you realize what's happening—poof! Socks in the same drawer, underwear neatly folded. I can't take *orderly*, Alex."

"I'm talking about the survival of your company as an organization and not your underwear," she said dryly.

"Oh, sure, that's how it will start, but I know what your goal is." He lowered his eyebrows. "You want to get into my skivvies."

Alex erupted in laughter. It was the first time he'd witnessed genuine joy in her expression, and it thrilled him that he was the cause.

"I'll let you have your delusion long enough for me to alphabetize your information," she said.

"I'll make a deal with you," he suggested. "I'll *consider* a new filing system if you agree to let me get you to and from work instead of using cabs and buses. Close your mouth, Alex."

"I'm perfectly capable of getting from point A to B without getting lost."

"I know you are, but this city has an increasing crime rate, and you're just a slip of a thing, the proverbial sitting duck for any nut who gets an idea. There's no need for you to keep going back and forth all alone when I'm willing to drive you."

"I've been taking care of myself for a while, JJ. I don't need a man looking after me." Her strident objection only made him more adamant.

"It's not a matter of you being able to look out for yourself, it's about not taking unnecessary risks. I was a cop for a few years, I know what can happen to a single woman traveling on her own. I'm not trying to be domineering, Alex, but I'm concerned." His speech ran down, and he held a breath expectantly. He hadn't wanted to scare her but he spoke the truth. A few women had disappeared when they'd stepped into an unlit area just for a second—and he'd seen, firsthand, the gruesome results. Nothing filled him with anxiety and horror as much as the thought of Alex getting hurt that way.

"Fine. You win."

"Thank you," he sighed.

"You can be grateful when I've straightened out your filing cabinets." With that parting shot, she smiled and scurried from the jeep.

JJ watched her go inside and mentally patted himself on the back. If the extra time he spent with her during those rides to and from work helped her to warm up to him a little more . . . well, that was an added bonus!

Alex lay in bed the next morning enjoying the last half hour of calm before Hank and Billy roused themselves. The house was quiet, the sun barely up as the digital clock on her nightstand flickered to seven.

A solid eight hours sleep had been easier to come by this week, and she had JJ to thank. The advance on her paycheck had covered a few overdue bills and two small gifts for her sons. For the first day in as long as she could remember, she woke with a smile.

On the ride home yesterday, she had felt comfortable discussing her family and her recent troubles. It had only been as she'd closed the door on his headlights that it had struck her how she'd rambled on selfishly, never once asking JJ about his own family. Not that she was entitled to any of his personal history, but it would have been the polite thing to do.

She yawned and stretched, letting those few unguarded moments in his arms resurface. He was a wonderful kisser, though she ought not to have let herself sink into the swirling abyss he'd created with his mouth and hands.

Alex groaned, recalling slapping him. She really felt awful about that. A simple *no, thank you* would have sufficed — it wasn't as if she hadn't responded with equal abandon, thus leading him to believe that she wanted the embrace to go on . . . and on . . .

"Behave!" she muttered to her heating body and got up to take a shower.

An hour later, she was dressed in faded jeans and an old fisherman's sweater, hair curling loosely around her shoulders while she made breakfast. Her mother and father were reading the morning paper over coffee, and the boys had settled down long enough to digest toast and eggs.

She was about to scramble some for herself when an engine rumbled in the driveway. Glancing out the window, she was stumped to see JJ coming up the short walk.

"Hi." He grinned sheepishly when she opened the door. "I know it's early but I thought you might need this." He waved the wallet she hadn't known she was missing under her nose. "It must have fallen out in the jeep or something."

Alex took the item from him slowly, trying to comprehend how it had gotten out of her purse. She distinctly recalled undoing the straps and the compartment for her keys last night. "That's odd," she remarked faintly and motioned him inside. "Anyway, it's a good thing you dropped it off. My life is in here. Have you had breakfast?" She hoped he didn't notice her hesitation. Inviting him to meet her family was an iffy move.

"Oh, I don't want to intrude." He looked uncertain, as if he had trouble trusting that she might want his company.

Perverse or not, she suddenly found that she did.

"No, really, come into the kitchen. I was just about to get some myself." She held out her hands for his jacket.

JJ shook hands with her father and nodded politely to her mother as he was introduced. He seemed even bigger in the tiny room, his body very large at the crowded table. Hank and Billy anxiously made room for him and now sat staring while he engaged in small talk with her parents.

"Are you a real p'ibate inbestigator?" Billy piped up, his mouth crammed with toast.

"Yes, I am."

"Like the one in Hawaii with the red car?"

"Aren't you a bit young to remember that show?"

Lorna explained, "He sneaks in to watch the reruns."

"Ah. Well, it's not nearly as exciting."

Billy chirped, "You got a gun?"

"No, I don't really need one. When I was a police officer I had one."

"Didja ever shoot anybody?"

Alex peered over her shoulder to see if he was annoyed by the questions. He was trying his best not to laugh if the glint in his eye was anything to go by.

"No, I never had cause to."

"Oh." The disappointment was obvious. "D'ya like Mom?"

Alex dropped a fork. "Billy, dear, eat your breakfast." She set a plate heaped with bacon and eggs in front of JJ and prepared one for herself.

"I like your mom just fine."

Was it her imagination, or had he smothered a chuckle?

"She gives good hugs." Billy noisily slurped his orange juice.

"He can't hug Mom," Hank cut in matter-of-factly. "He's just her boss."

"Benny's Mom *married* her boss."

"Billy, if you're finished, go make your bed." Alex was sure her hair was blushing.

JJ coughed discreetly as both boys left the table. "They're very articulate for their age."

"Sometimes a little too articulate."

George Eldrich squinted over the top of his bifocals. "Alex started reading to them when they were only six months old. There's no stopping them these days." He paused to scratch the top of his head. "I caught Hank a while back hauling everything out of the kitchen cupboards. When I asked what he was doing, he said he was checking the ingredients for chemical preservatives."

Laughter rumbled from JJ's chest, and Alex was relieved her long sleeves hid the goose bumps it caused.

"Our grandsons are exceptionally bright." Lorna was apparently smitten with their guest and proceeded to extol the virtues of her daughter and her sterling skills as a parent.

The daughter in question was having a tough time keeping her color down and tried to convey to the woman her embarrassment. Unfortunately, Lorna was on a roll, and short of kicking her under the table, there wasn't much Alex could do about it.

Two hours passed before JJ took his leave. After enjoying her discomfort—and she could see he was reveling in it—he accepted her father's invitation to sit in the living room for a chat. Tidbits of their conversation floated out to Alex while she cleared away the dishes. Her father had been fascinated to learn that her employer had played hockey in university. He proudly showed off his memorabilia, probing JJ for details about his sporting days.

Finally, he strolled back to the kitchen, blue eyes gleaming with an unholy light, dimples flashing as he attempted to conceal his glee. "I like your family. Your parents are extremely forthcoming."

She groaned and slumped in a chair. "I'm so sorry. You must be bored spitless."

"On the contrary, it was an enlightening experience." JJ leaned casually against the doorframe and folded his arms. "You never told me you were a Girl Guide."

"Okay, you've had your fun."

He chortled, feigning meanness. "Oh, I think I'm just getting started. Your mother is a veritable data bank."

"Be careful. She's been known to stretch the truth a little."

"Not as far as her only child is concerned. You're doing a great job with Hank and Billy. Some women would have folded long ago." Something bleak touched his eyes and was gone. He made a visible effort to banish the somber moment and dredged up his familiar grin. "I'll be leaving now, before your stress tolerance goes bust."

With a wry expression, Alex shook her head. "The real sources of my angst are in the other room."

He gave a low laugh. "You know your parents mean well."

"Yes, I s'pose. Thanks again for bringing my wallet." She saw him to the door and helped him with his coat, telling her itching hands not to linger on those magnificent shoulders.

"I'd ask you to supper but, aside from the fact that you'd turn me down, I promised Spike I'd cover his surveillance shift tonight. I will change your mind, however," he promised, tracing the line of her cheek with a blunt-tipped finger.

"JJ," she sighed in exasperation.

"Say that again," he murmured, looking over his shoulder. Then, apparently certain that no one was within hearing distance, he whispered, "Say my name in that husky voice." He brushed his mouth over hers.

"Tell me your name and I'll say it."

"J-A-Y J-A-Y."

She couldn't help but laugh quietly. "No. What's on your birth certificate? What does your mother call you?"

A stillness came over him, and she realized she'd hit a sore spot. "My mother only ever called me JJ. The joke she left on paper." His expression was shuttered, and his tone was tinged with bitterness. The reference to his mother in the past tense led her to believe she had passed away.

"I'm sorry, I didn't mean to pry."

"It's all right," he said, but clearly it wasn't. "She's been gone for quite some time."

Chapter Five

Sunday dawned cold and gray, much like JJ's spirits when he unlocked the door to his apartment.

Last night had been a long, tedious waste of time. For hours he'd sat in his cold jeep watching and waiting for a bail-jumping abusive husband to emerge from his girlfriend's house. No dice. The perp must have been tipped off by his mistress.

He'd spent half the night going back over his conversation with Alex—he hadn't acknowledged the huge gap between her upbringing and his until she'd nudged him with the question about his mother.

Suddenly, it had hit him like a sledgehammer that he had next to nothing in common with her—she'd been raised lovingly in a traditional environment and had gone on to marry and have kids of her own. It was like a natural pattern that most people followed. Normal people, with roots and relatives and some kind of structure to their lives. He, on the other hand, had been abandoned and left to drift from one foster home to another, never envisioning a future for himself that included anyone else. A solitary existence touched by only a handful of friends was what he'd decided his fate would be. He'd given up hoping for abiding love and acceptance at about the age of twelve.

What JJ knew about home, family, and enduring affection could fill a thimble halfway. Sure, he had close buddies like Jonas and Steven whom he considered practically brothers, but when it came to the numerous invitations extended from them to share holidays, he'd always turned them down. He recognized the sincerity with which the offers were made but he just could never shake the sensation of being on the outside looking in. Nance, bless her heart, had tried to draw him into the circle of her family, but with much the same result.

So, what all did he hope to accomplish by snooping around a sweet-faced widow and her adorable kids? He didn't have an answer, and that made his mood even blacker as he undressed and flaked out on his big, lonely bed.

A distant *ding-dong* interrupted his sleep. He lifted his face from the pillow and listened, trying to identify the origin of the persistent noise. It stopped promptly, and he gratefully buried his kisser once more, sinking back into unconscious bliss.

A high-pitched whir penetrated the fog surrounding his brain. Groaning, he fumbled blindly for the phone beside his bed. He knocked the receiver onto the floor and had to force an eyelid open and he leaned down to grab it.

"What?" he asked of the offending instrument and he flopped back on the pillow.

"JJ?"

"Do you know what time it is, Kincaid?" he rasped.

Steven replied heartily, "Past noon. Up and at 'em, buddy."

"It can't be that late, I only just got in bed."

"We brought lunch."

"Oh God. Please tell me you're not out in the hallway."

"Okay, Jonas and I aren't out in the hallway with pizza," he obliged loudly. "Now, come open the door."

JJ told him in no uncertain terms what to do with himself.

"Lazy squid," Steven remarked, and he disconnected the cell phone. Not a millisecond later, the doorbell began its *ding-donging* anew.

Yanking open the door in his boxer shorts, JJ groused, "Don't you guys have anyone else to bother?" and not expecting an answer, stomped into the kitchen.

Jonas tossed a jumbo box down on the table and shrugged out of his coat. "We've learned to ignore your rotten attitude in the morning. Don't drink from the carton." The comment was automatic, the redhead having spent four years of university keeping his roommates in line.

"Sorry, Mother," JJ replied, putting the empty container back in the fridge. "What brings you two out on such a dreary day?"

"I convinced Jonas that domesticity has its limits when I caught him braiding Viv's hair." Steven shoved a wayward brown lock off his forehead and reached for a slice of greasy pizza. "And there's a hockey game on at two."

"Of course. You, pizza, and hockey. I missed the connection," he said dryly. The three friends had been on the team in school. The Triple Threat was what the coach had dubbed them because of their effectiveness on the ice together.

"Late night?" Jonas enquired.

"Yeah. Stakeout." JJ dropped into a chair and made for the box.

"Surveillance on a Saturday night. Man, you've got to change professions." Steven stuffed a bit of crust in his mouth and sighed. "Nine to five is the key."

MK Electronics, the firm owned and operated by his friends, was thriving, and the success had finally allowed them to slow down a little. He could do the same if he wanted, but he often took stakeout duty to enable some of his married employees, like Spike, to get in quality time with their spouses and kids.

All innocence, Jonas asked, "How's Alex working out?"

"Great."

"That's it? Just *great*?"

"Mmm-hmm." He lifted a slice of the gastric nightmare and bit into it, staring blankly at the wall opposite. Around a mouthful, he added, "Wonderful."

"Did you ask her out again?" Steven grilled. "You seemed pretty chummy at the reception."

JJ discarded an anchovy in disgust.

"Well?"

"Butt out, Kincaid."

"Jonas, this matrimonial thing isn't contagious, is it?" Steven was the last unmarried brother in the Kincaid clan and claimed to be allergic to the phrase *I do*. JJ knew it was a bluff. Some people were just cut out for that stuff.

"You wanna marry Vanzant?" Jonas frowned.

"I meant—"

"Relax, boys, there's nothing between Alex and me." A straight face did come in handy.

"You had me worried. She's not your usual type." Steven wadded up the napkin he'd used and pitched it on the table.

Jonas picked it up and put it in the now empty box.

"What's that supposed to mean?" JJ demanded.

The other two men shared a look and simultaneously responded, "Celeste."

A busty amazon flashed before his eyes, and he exclaimed, "I never slept with her!"

They threw back their heads and roared with laughter.

"I swear, I did not sleep with that woman."

"How would you describe her, Steven?"

"Vacant."

"I never laid a hand on her!"

They shook their heads, still snickering.

"Honestly," JJ insisted. "Once, when she leaned over to whisper something in my ear—her breast fell out."

"So?" Steven gasped. "I'd have thought that'd be a turn-on."

"No, you don't understand. Her breast actually came loose and dropped onto the floor."

"An implant?" Jonas was wiping the tears from his brown eyes.

"A . . ." he searched for the term, "falsy? And I caught a glimpse of her genuine anatomy. It was hairy."

"Man hairy?" Steven queried faintly.

Nodding, he elaborated, "It turned out that Celeste was born *Cecil* and he'd not gotten his operation yet. Now, b'ys — stop laughin' — I'm pretty liberal but I couldn't go there."

After a long five minutes, the two sobered up.

"Well, I'll say this," Jonas complimented, deadpan, "you're becoming choosier."

"I'm mending my ways."

Alex fairly gawked at the older couple on her parents' doorstep. It had been two years since she'd seen her former in-laws — two years of not a single word except the occasional card for the boys.

Elizabeth Manning stood tall and stiff, her darkly dyed hair immaculate. She waited expectantly to be greeted. Her narrow eyes darted behind Alex, searching for signs of other life.

Gerard was a skinny, stooped man whom she'd once fancied had simply wilted from years spent with his wife. She'd often pitied the balding accountant, for he was clearly not a dominant force in the relationship.

"Well, Alex, aren't you going to ask us in?" Elizabeth demanded, imperious. "We've come a long way to visit our dear grandchildren."

"Considering Gander is in the same province, it's probably not so long when it comes to seeing relatives." But she held the door wide, and they entered, glancing around the small interior.

The Mannings had always looked down their noses at people who had less than they did. Although, truth be known, Alex thought their supposed wealth was highly exaggerated. Still, that had never stopped Elizabeth from criticizing the simple comfort of the Eldrich home. It was modest but it was warm and well cared-for. So, if the woman dared open her thin mouth to put it down, she'd —

"Are they here?" enquired Gerard. "We can't stay long," he explained nervously.

"Hank and Billy are next door with friends."

"Well, could you ring over and tell them we're here?" Elizabeth had made herself at home in the living room.

Grateful that her parents had gone to a late church service, Alex prodded, her tone rigid, "Why did you come? You haven't bothered with us since Darryl died."

"We've decided that because the boys are all we have left of our son, we ought to make a sincere effort to help with their upbringing." Her smile was deceptively bright, her eyes radiating a trace of hostility that couldn't be missed. Elizabeth had never liked her and made no bones about it. "Gerard and I brought them a few little things." She indicated the bags she was holding. "I'm sure they could use some new clothes and toys."

Knowing she couldn't, in good conscience, keep Hank and Billy from their father's family, Alex held her tongue and went to use the phone.

The next thirty minutes dragged like thirty years as she watched her sons rip open the flashily wrapped packages offered by their Grandma and Grandpa Manning. The clothes were miles too big, which gave Alex a cantankerous sense of satisfaction, but the toys were a hit.

Obviously unaccustomed to children, the couple made good their escape once they'd done their duty.

Hugely relieved when they headed for the door, Alex was nonetheless unable to conceal her shock when Elizabeth suggested, "Perhaps the boys would benefit from an extended visit to Gander — over the holidays?"

"Christmas is not a good time," she managed to get out. Did they honestly believe they could pop up after two years of ignoring the existence of their grandchildren and whisk them away for the most important time of the year? Even when Alex was penniless and without prospect of employment, she'd looked forward to making the Yuletide special for the boys. There was no way she'd be separated from them just to accommodate this snooty woman.

Elizabeth stared way down her patrician nose. "We can discuss it another time. Come along, Gerard."

Once they'd gone, Alex slumped against the door. What had prompted them to show an interest now? And why did it make her so uneasy? *Because Elizabeth Manning never did anything that didn't benefit her personally.*

She wondered what the woman was up to, and a cold dread washed over her.

Nance looked slightly flabbergasted. The pencil in her hair took a tumble, landing on her ample bosom when she planted her hands on her hips and glared across the office. "I found the perfect job for her, and you've changed your mind?"

JJ had surprised himself a little that morning when he'd peeked to his right in the jeep and realized how much he liked seeing Alex every day. He made the decision right then not to deprive himself of even a single moment with her.

She'd been more subdued than usual when he'd picked her up, and he'd sensed there was something heavy on her mind. He'd asked if anything was bothering her, but she'd only shrugged and said, "It's nothing", so he'd let it drop. By the time they'd pulled into his parking space, he'd wangled a small smile out of her.

"Sorry to have wasted your time, Nance. I think I can handle myself with Alex just fine without shipping her off to another job." He leaned back in his chair and waited for her to lecture him about sending people on useless errands.

Instead, she said, "I hope you know what you're doing. Sexual harassment is in the news a lot these days."

"I've been over that with her. I think she understands her position is safe whether or not anything develops between us. I promised I'd behave in the office." He paused. "*You* don't believe I'd ever—"

Nance cut him off with a bark of laughter. "I know you're a pussy cat, hon. I just want to be sure Alex knows it, too."

"I am touched by your concern."

"Uh-huh. Is it my imagination, or is she *awfully* quiet this morning? I mean, she's not a gabber but normally she shows an interest in conversation."

JJ blew out a breath. "You've noticed. I couldn't get it out of her, but something's on her mind."

"Have lunch with her. I don't think she's used to sharing her troubles with anyone, and since you're *so* interested . . ."

"Yeah, whatever. Don't you have work to do?" He grinned cheekily. "I am the boss, after all. You shouldn't be bending my important ear like this."

Nance blew him a raspberry and slammed the door on her way out.

Lunch time, he found Alex in the cafeteria and slid his tray onto the table next to hers. "Are you planning to eat that sandwich or just play with it?"

"I was thinking I might bring it back and give it to the kids to use as home base," she said dully.

"Tough?"

She tapped the bread against her tray. "It's a little too

firm, yes."

"There's a small restaurant down the street. You could start going there."

Alex shook her head. "Takes too long for lunch. Besides, the food here is decent enough if you don't happen to get a week-old sandwich from the vending machine. I wasn't hungry for the real food."

"You'll lose those precious three pounds you've gained if you don't eat something." He'd noticed that her slim body had gotten a bit softer around the edges. Her face, too, hadn't seemed as pale as when they'd first met. "Do you want to talk about it?"

She darted him a glance and looked sheepish. "Is it that obvious?"

JJ took a giant bite out of his cheeseburger and nodded.

Alex sighed and told him briefly that her late husband's parents had made an impromptu visit the day before. They sounded like snobs to him, having dealt with his share growing up as a poor orphan. When she finished the story, she folded her dainty hands on the table and watched him absently. The lost expression on her face touched something deep within him, and he wanted nothing more than to make it go away.

"This was probably just an impulse on their part, Alex. Maybe they won't show up again. Is this Elizabeth person so difficult?"

"It's not simply that she's hard to get along with. She makes me feel like I'm a rotten mother—"

"That's ridiculous," he stated firmly. "Anyone who sees you with your sons can tell how devoted you are."

"But I've barely been able to put clothes on their back, let alone give them hand-held video games."

JJ couldn't stand the defeated slump of her shoulders. Covering her hands with his, he solemnly declared, "You know what's important to your kids, Alex. It's not the things you buy for them that they'll remember and thank you for later, it's the goodnight hugs and kisses and the bedtime stories. Take it from someone who was raised by the Province of Newfoundland and Labrador, no child really appreciates the creature comforts as much as the love of good family." He gently thumbed a tear from beneath her eye.

Sniffing inelegantly, she met his gaze. "I know what you're saying is true, but—Province of Newfoundland and Labrador?"

"Foster care. I was bumped around from one well-meaning household to another, and believe me, sweetheart, nobody ever cared for me the way you do for Hank and Billy. You should be proud of how you've taken care of them. Don't let some snotty woman make you think differently." He stopped, for the first time seeing the cafeteria was nearly deserted.

Alex grimaced. "I'd better get back to work or the boss'll fire me." She seemed to hesitate, but then she leaned over and planted a kiss on his rugged cheek. "Thanks for the pep talk. I needed it."

Wondering if he should have told her about his childhood, he stared after her retreating figure and touched his cheek. If his disclosure helped erase the haunted look from those lovely eyes, then it was well worth it.

That impulsive gesture stayed with him for the rest of the day, the spot where she'd kissed him still tingling. Several times he stalled in his thought process to relive the cherished moment, once even spacing out on Jerry as he tried to explain his newest idea for a security system. Finally, he gave up concentrating altogether when she stepped on the elevator with him and smiled.

"You got a lot done today," she remarked.

The doors closed on the two of them.

"Mmm," said his stupid mouth. He punched the button for the main lobby. "Not as much as I'd have liked." His briefcase was full of the work she'd distracted him from. The ride home was going to be dicey—all those traffic lights and other vehicles to pay attention to.

Suddenly, the elevator halted, the unexpected jolt throwing them both off-balance. After he checked to make sure Alex was all right, JJ's gaze flew to the board indicating the floor numbers. The light flickered from three to four and back again, as if it couldn't decide what level the car was on.

"Oh, no," his companion sighed, "we're stuck in between."

"No, we're not." He jabbed at the buttons in agitation. "We can't be." The phone behind the emergency panel was dead, and his movements grew frantic because the elevator seemed to be shrinking. The lights dimmed abruptly, a signal that there was a power outage and the building's generator had kicked in.

An invisible belt tightened around his chest, restricting his airway. His face went hot, then cold, the blood racing to his head and away. The sound of rushing water was in his ears, and he put his hands up to block it, knowing the thunderous racket would not cease until he got out of the hellishly tiny box. The world tilted, and he swayed on his feet.

Then, Alex smacked him. Vaguely, he pondered how such a delicate hand could deliver a blow that hard—again.

"Breathe, JJ!" She dragged his hands down and instructed, "In through your nose and out through your mouth. That's better. Just breathe."

"You should know I'm claustrophobic." The dizziness had receded somewhat, but he was still struggling to get more oxygen.

She loosened his tie and worriedly asked, "Does anything help?"

"Nothing."

"I'm sure we won't be here long." The statement was optimistically voiced.

"The power's out, Alex. There's no telling how long we'll be stuck in this godforsaken can!" He began to hyperventilate all over again.

"Pretend you're somewhere else."

"That doesn't work."

"Then put your arms around me and close your eyes."

"What?" he asked in confusion.

"Just do it." She pulled his arms over her shoulders and gripped his waist. "I hope this works, JJ. You look terrible." And, so saying, she stretched upward and planted her lips on his.

For what seemed like an eternity, Alex worked her mouth against his, trying to coax a response. His body was rigid, the line of his shoulders rock-hard. Just then she thought she might as well give up, but he relaxed a trifle and tentatively kissed her back.

JJ's big hands slid down her spine and pressed her snugly to him. She let her eyes drift shut and savored the feel of his strong embrace, winding her arms around his back. He drew her with him and leaned on the wall and settled comfortably, never breaking the intimate contact. His mouth opened wider, and he slanted his head to go deeper, driving his tongue inside. She suckled while he stroked her, and she wasn't even aware of shoving his sweater up until she felt warm, smooth skin. He groaned, and she found the pebbled nipples in the coarse hair of his chest and rubbed them urgently, all sane thought dissipating because her excitement was so fueled by his.

Dazed, Alex didn't object at all when his hand moved to

grasp her behind. He pressed his pelvis into her, the bulge of his arousal erotically prominent as it touched her belly. Unthinking, she cupped the steely ridge of his pants. His body jerked in response, he tore his mouth free, breathing harshly, and he threw his blond head back. The exposed column of his neck was too tempting to ignore, so she tenderly scraped it with her teeth and then laved the abrasion hotly.

Completely caught up in pleasing him, she froze guiltily upon hearing an older woman's voice say, "Oh, forgive me. I can see this elevator's taken." The doors swished closed again, leaving her to face the humiliation of having been seen mauling her boss.

"Well, you certainly diverted my attention." JJ's raspy comment did nothing to lessen her embarrassment.

Alex mumbled into the curve of his neck, "I've probably given that old lady a stroke." She moved away from him and bent to retrieve the purse and gloves she'd abandoned. Avoiding his sapphire gaze, she handed him his briefcase and hit the button to continue the ride to the main lobby.

"I don't think she saw anything, Alex. Our coats were disguising your questing hands more than adequately." He hadn't budged from his position against the wall, and his eyes were still glazed with passion. "You may have to carry me to the parking area, as walking will pose a problem."

She closed her eyes, plainly remorseful whilst flaming heat seemed to fill her entire body. "I am *so very, very sorry*. I was only trying to take your mind off being closed in here."

A wicked chuckle rumbled deep in his chest. "You definitely succeeded. I'm greatly flattered that you got so carried away. I don't recall ever having an attractive female launch herself at me with such *zeal* before."

Alex zipped across the lobby and down the corridor leading to the garage as if the Devil were at her heels. She was composing herself admirably as she stood next to the jeep and watched him stroll up beside her. The demon then had the nerve to shatter it when he stooped over and smacked a warm smooch on her.

"We're going to finish what almost happened back there." His words held the ring of a promise, not a warning or a threat. "I'll have to remember to stop by the security office soon and see if the camera in the elevator went out with the power. You never know about these things." He smirked at her appalled expression. "Yes, Alex, there is probably a video tape somewhere in the building with our names on it."

"Oh . . . my . . . *God!*"

"Don't fret. The system is one of ours. I'll take care of the tape—if there is one."

"That really was inappropriate." She cringed at the thought of a very bored security guard getting more of an eyeful than the anonymous elderly lady had.

"Mmm." JJ studied her intently, his expression inscrutable. "I want you, Alex. I know you want me, too."

They both knew she'd be lying if she tried denying it, so she remained silent.

"I'm not talking about a one-nighter to scratch an itch. I care about you."

When she just looked at him helplessly, he unlocked the passenger door. Before she turned to get in, he brushed his mouth fleetingly across hers. The action was so sweet and careful that an ache blossomed in her soul, a yearning for this strong, beautiful man that she couldn't ignore.

"Would you like to have dinner with us?" she surprised herself by asking.

"I wouldn't want to put your mother to any trouble."

"She won't mind. My parents are already devoted fans of yours."

He searched her face thoughtfully. "What about their daughter?"

"She's . . . ah . . . getting used to you." Alex smiled.

JJ nodded and quietly asserted, "I'll have to work on that."

And he did, accepting invitations from Alex and her family every evening that week. He stayed long after dinner was over and helped wash dishes. He played chess with George, proving himself a worthy opponent, and he read to Hank and Billy when they pleaded with their mother for one more story, thus lengthening his visits. He was patient and kind, as well as funny and brilliant.

Everyone adored him, especially Alex, and it scared her a little.

What frightened the bejeebers out of her, however, was the second visit from Elizabeth and Gerard. They came by the house that Thursday evening, long after JJ had left and the boys had gone to bed. The lateness of the hour and the sternly superior look on her mother-in-law's face put Alex on alert.

"We wanted to talk with you about the children in private," Elizabeth announced arrogantly.

Folding her arms, Alex decided it would be a mistake to let them past the porch door and said pointedly, "Then lower your voice or you'll wake them."

"You must realize, dear, that Gerard and I are better able to provide for the boys than you are. Child-rearing these days is so expensive, after all. We've discussed it at length and have agreed that we should be responsible for their welfare." Disregarding Alex's gaping mouth, she went on, "You're a young woman, and certainly you must miss having a social life, being burdened with the responsibility of motherhood. We can assume guardianship of the boys and move them to Gander with us. You'll be welcome to visit, of course, as long as it doesn't interfere with their studies. Think about it." Turning, the older woman summoned her quiescent spouse and departed airily.

76

CHAPTER SIX

"Go home, Alex." JJ had watched the object of his desire battle with a dire case of preoccupation all morning. She was evidently courting a raging headache, and the circles under her eyes told the tale of a sleepless night. *Damn her screwy in-laws!*

"I can't. I'm into the Ws and if I stop now I'll lose my place."

"Forget the files," he ordered as he gripped the armrests on her swivel chair and peered at her tired face. "You need to get some rest and stop worrying about those snobbish idiots."

"JJ, it's only noon."

"Go home and lie down. You'll need your rest for tonight."

"Tonight?"

He covertly glanced around to make sure no one was witnessing his attentive chat with the secretary. "I'm taking you out to a nice, quiet restaurant."

She groaned in protest.

"I refuse to take no for an answer. You deserve a break, some time for yourself. What better way to spend it than with a charming, witty, attractive companion?" That elicited a small smile.

"You're full of it."

"Guilty as charged." He nudged her pert nose with his. "Go home, rest up, and put on something sexy."

"I don't do *sexy*," she said wearily.

"Your breathing is sexy."

"I don't have a sitter. It's my parents' bridge night."

"Let me take care of it." *And whatever else that causes you trouble.*

Alex inhaled deeply. "You don't have to cheer me up. I'm sure you'd rather be spending your Friday night doing . . . *something.*"

"I'll be spending it with an adorable, sweet, sexy woman."

She gazed at him from beneath dark lashes. "Okay."

"I'll pick you up at seven." He called a cab for her and insisted on paying the fare. "Have the kids ready when I get there. We'll drop them off." Grinning goofily, he closed the door on her and waved as the car pulled away from the curb.

He strode purposely back to his office. He couldn't remember being this excited about a simple dinner date since—well, he'd never been this excited by the prospect of spending a few hours with a woman in a public place. Hell, he'd never been so charged at the prospect of an evening that he knew would end up in a bedroom.

Getting Alex into bed was something he anticipated with every waking breath, but he had no intention of pressing for that tonight. No, he just wanted to distract her from the apprehension caused by the Mannings, make her smile for him over a candlelight meal, and hopefully charm a goodnight kiss out of her. But that was it. He'd be the consummate gentleman and keep his covetous hands off her delectable person.

JJ hit the speed dial on his phone and leaned back as his friend's secretary greeted him and transferred the call.

"Mackenzie here." The redhead's baritone sounded distracted.

"Am I interrupting something, or can you spare a second for the guy who got you through post-secondary education?"

A grunt echoed in his ear. "Professor Maitland?"

"Funny, Jonas. You're a real funny man."

"I have a few minutes. What's on your mind?"

JJ cleared his throat. "I was wondering if you had plans this evening."

"Why, Vanzant, I didn't know you cared. I'm afraid you'll have to get through my wife, she's an extremely possessive woman."

"I wouldn't have your mug on a platter. I need a babysitter." He waited for the laughter to subside before continuing. "For Hank and Billy."

"Thank God. The image of your kids struck me as rather odd for some reason. You haven't been holding out, have you? I mean, with your track record, there could be a few little Vanzants running around." The laughter rumbled again.

"I'm offended. I have *never ever* taken any chances with my health and certainly not with fatherhood. And I'm not promiscuous," he added firmly. It was true, he'd made certain that he always used protection whether his sex partner said she was on the pill or not. Apart from the various diseases being passed about, he'd wanted to avoid bringing a child into the world who would have him for a father. That was a role he'd considered himself ill-equipped for.

"I'm kidding." Jonas sobered up. "I think Viv would love to take the boys for a few hours. As far as I know, we don't have anything on. Big date?"

"Not really," he lied. It was an important occasion in his mind, but probably not for Alex. "I just think she could do with a night out."

"Uh-huh," was the slow reply.

"Just dinner."

"Mmm-hmm. Rose's is very romantic."

JJ balked, "Who mentioned romance?"

"I do believe you're sinking. We'll take the kids." Jonas' dry chuckle reached him before the line was disconnected.

He grinned to himself and called directory assistance for the number to Rose's restaurant.

It was late in the afternoon when Viv called to say she would pick Hank and Billy up and keep them overnight. "I figured it was easier than carting them back home half asleep. I already spoke with Alex. She told me about her in-laws."

"*Former* in-laws," he corrected.

She laughed softly. "My, my. Don't you sound just a tad territorial?"

"Well, they have no business coming around and questioning her suitability as a parent after two years of disinterest."

"I agree. It's good that you're taking her out. But you'd better be careful."

Aggrieved, he exclaimed, "What am I, the Big Bad Wolf or something?"

"Or something," Viv wryly affirmed.

"I'm not going to push. She deserves better." The conversation was slightly embarrassing, but he wanted Viv to understand that he cared about her friend. In a way, he needed her approval, some hint that she considered him worthy of Alex. That was a notion he hadn't concerned himself with in the past—people could take him or leave him just as he was, and it had never once bothered him.

"You behave," warned Viv, but he sensed she was smiling, and that went a long way toward easing his apprehension.

"I will. Of course, if she decides she wants more than dinner—"

Viv hung up on him. She did that a lot.

The soft woolen material of her dress swished about her legs as she turned one way and then the other, the forest green color complementing her dark hair and eyes. It was full length and fastened in the back by a row of tiny buttons. The material hugged her breasts appealingly, the neckline dipping to reveal a tantalizing glimpse of creamy flesh. She idly speculated that her bare arms might draw the cold but dismissed the idea, knowing they'd be inside the cozy warmth of the restaurant. The outfit wasn't new, but she'd only worn it once, and the few pounds she'd gained allowed her to fill it out quite nicely again.

She wore no jewelry except a simple gold pendant her parents had given when she'd graduated high school.

Her hair had been left to tumble wildly about her shoulders, and only a touch of mascara and lip gloss enhanced her features.

She critically surveyed herself in the mirror one last time and was satisfied that she looked very feminine, if not sexy. Hopefully, JJ wouldn't find her lacking in comparison to his other dates.

The expression on his face said she needn't have tormented herself with that nagging question when she walked into the living room. He rose slowly from the couch, his intense blue gaze sweeping her from head to toe with blatant male appreciation.

He didn't appear too shabby either. The coal black suit was impeccably cut, the precise lines showing off the breathtaking width of his shoulders, and his red silk tie was knotted expertly over a blindingly white shirt. His curly blond hair was still a bit damp from his shower, and he smiled broadly, displaying those fascinating dimples and flawless teeth.

"You're beautiful," JJ murmured deeply, "but then, you always are." He held open her coat, and she slipped into it, a flutter in the pit of her stomach when his hands lingered.

"Flattery will get you nowhere."

He turned her toward him and pulled the lapels together, his eyes straying heatedly to her parted lips. "Ah, but flattery is usually insincere, and believe me, I'm very sincere." He retrieved his overcoat from the arm of the couch and shrugged it on. "I hope you don't mind that I told your parents not to wait up. They've already left for their bridge party."

Alex shook her head and preceded him to the door. He waited while she locked it and escorted her to the car. The black sedan belonged to Jonas, and she realized he'd swapped the jeep in consideration for her comfort, his own vehicle a little incompatible with an elegant night out.

They were seated promptly at the exclusive restaurant. Alex was again aware of the stares her companion drew as men and women alike appreciated the power and grace with which he moved.

The table JJ had reserved was tucked in a small alcove surrounded by a lattice wall on three sides. The greenery placed strategically amongst the diners created an intimately private atmosphere, a poinsettia plant here and there to tastefully mark the Christmas season. Candlelight illuminated the room effectively and seemed to lull everyone into communicating with mere whispers.

"This is lovely." Alex glanced around, for the first time noticing a dance floor the size of a postage stamp. A few couples swayed to the music dreamily, apparently caught up in the fanciful atmosphere.

"Would you like to dance?" he enquired, following the direction of her gaze. When she nodded, he reached for her hand and guided her to the floor. He held her loosely in the circle of his arms and smiled softly, his eyes darkening when she moved closer.

Alex let her lids drift down and leaned her head against his chest trustingly. One song flowed into the next, the sweet melodies washing over them whimsically.

JJ's heart thumped steadily in her ear, the rhythmic cadence soothing her worries away. Dimly, she registered that it quickened almost insignificantly when he bent to brush his lips to her temple, then her cheek.

The number faded, and they reluctantly separated and went back to their table.

Alex sipped from her wineglass and attempted to cool her raging emotions. How was it that this man could transport her to a place of serenity one minute and in the next, stir up unfamiliar feelings that had her wanting to get him out of those expensively tailored clothes?

"All right?" prodded the splendid man. "You look a bit flushed."

"It's the wine. I'm not much of a drinker." It wasn't a lie, but in this instance, it proved a welcome excuse.

"That makes two of us. I used to go on benders in university with the guys, but I found the mornings after weren't worth the trouble." He paused and then seemed to come to a decision. "My mother had a problem with alcohol, so I don't like to pass a limit of two drinks on a special occasion. A little wine with dinner or a scattered beer is all I normally imbibe."

"I did notice that at Jonas and Viv's wedding." A glass of wine and a half glass of liquor was all he'd drunk. Resolving to learn more about him, she probed hesitantly, "Do you remember much about your mother?"

He twirled the glass, collecting his thoughts. "Not a lot. I was eight when she dropped me at the orphanage and took off with her latest boyfriend. I only remember that she slept when she wasn't drinking and would rather go hungry than thirsty."

"Is she still living?"

"No, I tracked her down some years ago out of curiosity. She'd been killed in a car accident in PEI—driving drunk." JJ's voice was cool and detached, as if he'd mourned the loss of the woman long before he'd learned of her death.

"What about your father?" Alex asked in a gentle voice, afraid to push him into silence with such a personal interrogation. She wanted to know about how he grew up, what he'd felt and experienced, and how he managed to turn out just fine without the love and support she'd always taken for granted.

"There was no name on my birth certificate. I doubt if she knew who he was, or which one," he replied, dry. "Mother was a little generous in that department. Anyway, I was fostered out to several families until I turned eighteen. That's how I met Nance—we happened to be placed in the same house for a year. I was ten or eleven, I think."

Alex's heart ached for the little boy he'd been, but she tried not to let it show. He might mistake her compassion for pity and he was too proud to put up with that.

"Anyway, I busted my butt in high school and landed a few scholarships. Hockey kept me in university for four years. I spent a year at the police academy and walked a beat for a couple more. Then I figured I'd be happier working as a PI and got a job with an ex-cop. I saved and took out loans to start up on my own six years ago and—voila! Here I am, boring you to death with my life story." JJ grinned and flashed his dimples. "I'm supposed to be distracting you with my charm, not relating ancient history."

"I like hearing about you."

"Well," he said, opening a menu, "I've never been all that comfortable talking about my personal business. Not that I mind telling you . . ." He laughed. "Actually, I really *don't* mind discussing private stuff with you."

Alex smiled in relief. She hoped he continued to be so at ease with her.

The waiter appeared to take their orders, then tactfully withdrew.

"So, tell be about Alex Manning."

"You know about me," she dismissed.

"Not really. I don't know how you met your husband or if you intend to remarry one day—"

"No." She nearly choked on her wine. She had no plans to tie herself to a man ever again. Extricating her life from Darryl's had taught her a valuable lesson—never depend on someone else to fulfill your needs or fool yourself into believing they're concerned with anything but their own.

JJ was silent for a long time. "Did you love him that much?"

Love. Alex wondered if she'd ever really loved Darryl or if she'd been infatuated with the idea of it, bowled over by his promises of the perfect life together.

"We met in college. We married at twenty-one. I got pregnant with Hank, and he convinced me to drop out of school and stay home." She sketched out the bare details automatically, loath to lay out her disillusion and humiliation. "Let's just say I don't want to be dependent on anyone that way again. It takes too much of me to pick up the pieces when they can't be relied on."

"His death must have been hard on you." JJ lowered his eyes to the centerpiece and idly touched the sprigs of holly and mistletoe surrounding a fat, white candle.

She watched his long fingers, mesmerized momentarily by the unmistakable strength in them, a strength that was as much a part of the man himself as his blond hair or his endearing grin. Not like her late husband, who'd not only given in to his weaknesses, but had used any excuse he could think of to justify the behaviour.

"It was a long two years," she finally said. It had been that. Darryl's parents had contributed minimally to his care and visited only long enough to complain that Alex wasn't doing much for him, that he looked so dreadful that Elizabeth couldn't bear to watch him *wasting away.*

"I'm sorry." His quietly spoken words roused her from the past, and she smiled sheepishly.

"Let's change the subject. Tell me about your youthful escapades." She sat back and laughed through the first and second course as he described Jonas rescuing him and Steven from getting arrested when they'd started a brawl outside the campus pub. Then the redhead had invited the two to share his apartment, thereby saving them rent money. Lastly, he made her giggle so hard that she was forced to cover her mouth when he told her how he and Steven had almost blown up said apartment by attempting to bake a casserole.

"I wanted to follow the recipe, but Stevie got creative. Jonas warned us after that not to go near the kitchen. He took over the cooking. We just ate with our heads down and thanked God at least one of us knew what he was doing." JJ drank from his water glass and hefted a forkful of linguine. "You said you dropped out of school when you became pregnant. What were you studying?"

"I wanted to be a teacher."

"Do you ever think about going back? You're great with kids. Besides Hank and Billy, I noticed how well you handled Spike's little girls when they came by the office. You have a natural talent for restoring order where there is none."

Alex was touched by the compliment. "I'd love to finish my degree, but circumstances haven't permitted me the luxury. I do love kids. I had hoped to teach at the middle level—that's where a lot of children lose interest or don't get the encouragement they need to keep at it."

"Maybe you'll get back someday."

She lifted a shoulder half-heartedly. "We'll see."

They danced again while they waited for dessert to arrive, comfortably wrapped in each other's arms as if they'd done it countless times before. Alex tried to keep her traitorous body from letting him see just how deeply his nearness affected her. But her breasts throbbed and her breathing grew shallow as she fought to remain indifferent to the invitingly masculine warmth of him.

"Alex?" he whispered.

"Mmm?"

His hands slid down her back and pressed her more intimately to him, his very aroused body electrifying her senses. "I only meant this evening to include supper and conversation, honestly. But if you wanted—"

"Yes."

"—to go back to my place—"

"Yes, JJ."

"—then I'm open to—*yes?*"

She pulled back and stared up at him solemnly. "I want you to take me home to your apartment."

Closing his eyes, he exhaled slowly. When he looked at her next, it was with the most naked, vulnerable expression she'd ever seen. "Are you sure?"

"Absolutely. I want you." She wet her lips. "I want to be with you."

He swallowed visibly. "Then I guess we'll skip dessert?"

Negotiating traffic was probably not the thing to be doing when in this condition, JJ hypothesized. But then, he'd managed dancing, walking, chewing, and forming complete sentences all evening while courting a bothersome ache that hollered for attention.

He was certain that damned waiter knew just how he suffered because the guy had worn a smirk every time he'd hovered next to Alex, ostensibly to advise her on her choice of entree. Did the man have no sympathy for members of his own gender? It was unfortunate that men were cursed with the kind of anatomy that allowed others to easily discern when they'd been struck with a case of unsatisfied physical hunger.

Women, on the other hand, had no difficulty disguising when they were in a bad way. At any rate, a man couldn't be entirely sure until her clothes were off. Of course, if she stared at you with enormous brown eyes that blazed hotter than an inferno and asked you to take her home, well, how could you miss the signs?

JJ was accustomed to women being bold and audacious when it came to letting a man know what they wanted. He was also used to women playing coy and trying to soften their messages with a flutter of eyelashes or a turned-aside stare. Alex had done neither. Instead, the simple honesty of her words had pierced his soul when she'd said she wanted to be with him. Her eyes were soft and luminous and a little anxious, perhaps because she really wasn't certain of his response. That she wanted him badly enough to risk rejection was humbling to him.

He hadn't expected to tell her about his mother or growing up a ward of the province, and he felt a bit odd that it hadn't stirred up unpleasant memories. In the past, he had avoided relating the information to women he'd dated. If they'd started asking about personal matters, he'd always changed the subject. He'd become very adept at steering conversations away from himself. That he hadn't fallen back on his habit of doing so with Alex was a marvel.

JJ pulled the sedan into his parking space and killed the lights. Silence filled the interior as they both stared through the windshield. He cleared his suddenly tight throat, and she jumped. "If you'd rather go home, I'll understand. There's no pressure, Alex."

She held his gaze for a moment. "No. I want this to happen. I want something for myself, for us, even if it's just one night."

"One night won't be enough." A thousand nights wouldn't satisfy the longing he had for this woman. He'd be lying if he told himself it was only about sex, that he could take her to bed and be done with it. He wouldn't call what he felt *love* because he had no experience with the phenomenon — wasn't sure it even existed — but it damn well wasn't simply lust. *That* he could relate to.

"I can't get involved in a relationship right now, JJ. My life is too . . . *confused*."

"I'm not expecting any promises," he assured her. "Just don't shut the door on the possibility down the road."

Alex laughed softly. "Aren't you the one who referred to love and commitment as *tripe* a couple of weeks ago?"

"I believe it was *claptrap*, and I'm not hinting at marriage. You did say you never wanted to try that again." The notion that she didn't consider him a viable candidate for husbandry niggled at him, but he dismissed it as an ego thing.

"No, one go round the matrimonial circle was sufficient."

JJ grinned. "Now that we've settled that, would you like to go up?"

The apartment was on the second floor of a restored house, the area having been renovated to meet the demand of the offshore oil industry. The place where he lived was decorated sparsely and was a touch incongruous with the cozy design of the house. He was a bit ashamed that his walls held no photographs of friends or that his glass coffee tables weren't covered with magazines. The place appeared modern and spotless, as if nobody lived there. Strange, he pondered for the first time since moving his things there two years ago, how he thought of the apartment in the same context he had foster homes — it was just a transient place to eat and sleep before moving on.

Alex laid her coat on a chair and scanned the living room. "Nice place."

"No, it isn't," he said, recognizing the truth.

"It *is* a bit . . . um . . . cool."

"I was thinking *sterile*. I guess I've never looked at it from anyone else's vantage point." He shed his suit jacket and moved toward her. Lifting a silky strand of black hair, he noted, "The room seems a lot less austere with you in it."

She fastened a hand around his wrist and pressed warm lips to his palm. "Are you going to kiss me anytime soon?"

The ache in his groin intensified, and he drew in a ragged breath. "Don't you want to move into the bedroom?"

"Later," Alex whispered, reaching for his tie.

He stood transfixed as she divested him of his shirt next and stopped to stare at his naked chest, sliding her fingers through the blond hair covering his pecs and arrowing down his taut stomach. She traced every ridge of muscle as if fascinated and brushed his nipples with a volatile flick of her thumbs.

Catching her hands before they arrived at this belt buckle, he led her to the long sectional couch and gently pushed her down. He knelt then and removed her high-heeled boots, tossing them aside and slipping trembling hands beneath her dress to travel the length of her legs, stopping only when he found the release on her stockings. He watched her closely in the semi-darkness and deftly removed them, throwing the silky things after her boots.

Alex nestled a dainty foot on his thigh and proceeded to inch closer to his throbbing erection. He held his breath when she reached her goal and massaged him erotically, likewise locking her heavy-lidded gaze with his.

"Easy, sweetheart," JJ groaned. "It won't take much of that before I . . . oh . . . a little more."

She scooted to the edge of the couch and covered his mouth hungrily with hers, framing his flushed face with those delightfully delicate hands. He shoved his own underneath her dress once more and cupped the heated center of her body through her panties. She arched into him and whimpered, the sexy sound pushing him past the limit of restraint. He fumbled around her hips and ripped the fabric barrier, at the same time yanking on his belt and zipper.

Their breathing was harsh when he searched his wallet and retrieved the foil packet, hurriedly making himself ready for her. He brought her as close to the edge of the sofa as he dared, dipping one finger inside to test her heat. She was tight and slick, and he was convinced that if he held back any longer he'd embarrass himself.

"JJ," Alex pleaded, tearing her mouth from his, "hurry."

"I know, baby. I feel it, too. Look at me," he rasped and shifted her from the couch onto his lap so she straddled him.

He gripped her soft bottom and drove upward, his penetration swift and deep. Alex cried out and threw her head back, the pure ecstasy in her expression thrilling to the essence of his soul. He stayed unmoving until she opened her eyes and smiled, her gaze sweet and wild at the same time.

"Okay?" JJ searched her face.

"Mmm-hmm." She raised up on her knees and sank down on him again. "You're perfect."

"Forgive me, if I can't" — she kissed his neck — "last" — her tongue darted inside the shell of his ear — "long." He gave in and thrust frantically, her throaty laugh spurring him on as he buried his shaft to the hilt over and over, each stroke bringing him dangerously close to climax.

Alex dug her nails into the flesh of his back and screamed, riding the waves of pleasure just when he erupted in mind-shattering release, the likes of which he'd never experienced.

When the fog lifted and he considered himself fit to stand, JJ managed to get them into his bedroom and remove the rest of their clothes. He lay her limp body on the king-sized bed and studied her in the lamplight. The dark cloud of hair spilling over his pillow looked right somehow. He slipped in beside her, tucking the blankets around her more securely while he watched her sleep. Black lashes lay against cheeks still flushed from lovemaking, her full mouth swollen and red from his kisses. He'd never seen a woman more beautiful than she was right now, in his bed.

"You're doing it again," Alex murmured, drowsy.

"What?"

"Staring. You do that a lot."

"I just realized," he said conversationally, "that I didn't once get to touch your breasts."

She slitted her eyes and worked her arms free, raising them above her on the pillow. The sheets slid off with the motion, revealing the full glory of her perfectly rounded globes. The rosy nipples tightened, and he sucked in a breath.

"I'd hate to think I'd deprived you."

"Witch," he scolded feebly, his burgeoning manhood bumping her hip. "What am I going to do with you?"

"Whatever you come up with, could we do it slowly this time? I want you inside me for as long as we can stand it."

"My God, Alex," he muttered, hoarse, "do you know what you're doing to me?"

Not waiting for an answer, he molded his hands to her breasts and squeezed rhythmically. Her breathing quickened, and he bent his head to take one dusky tip into his mouth, suckling ravenously when she arched her back and moaned. Transferring his attention to the other crest, he did the same and then, feeling the urgent coaxing of her hands clutching his hair, he took her more fully into his mouth and teased with the blistering heat of his tongue.

Taking a firm grip on her wrists, he anchored them down above her head as he kissed her deeply. She writhed, trying to join her body with his, but he pinned her with his more considerable weight.

"You wanted it slow, darling," he reminded her wickedly. "This could take hours."

She eased her arms down and placed them around his neck, smoothing her palms across broad shoulders slick with sweat. The sign of relenting had him smiling. She could set him off if she chose and she knew it, but she wanted to indulge in the rapture as badly as he.

"Tell me what it stands for." Her mild command reached him just when he nipped the lobe of an exquisitely shaped ear.

"Uh-uh."

"I'll guess."

JJ said against her parted lips, "No one ever calls me anything but . . ."

"J-A-Y J-A-Y."

"Mmm."

"No one at all?" She kissed a shoulder.

"Not even my mother."

"Just tell me the first . . . uh . . ."

He distracted her by slipping a hand between them and rubbing that hidden spot repeatedly.

"Just the first . . ." She bucked off the mattress.

"If I tell you," he whispered when she settled down, "you have to keep it a secret."

"I will."

"Jesse."

Alex bit her lip. "Jesse. *Jesse James?*"

He groaned. "I told you she had a warped sense of humor."

"Oh, I am sorry."

"Go ahead, laugh."

Although her eyes were brimming with mirth, not one giggle escaped. Instead, she told him, "I like Jesse. It sounds fascinating. I'll forget the other part."

"I'd be grateful." He kissed her again and reached inside the nightstand.

"Do you mind if I call you by your name in private?" she asked and watched him roll on a condom.

Positioned between her thighs, he cautioned, "If no one else is around." He liked the way she said his name, and she proceeded to do so, speaking it very softly as he entered the tight sheath of her and pumped with maddening slowness.

Later, when he'd eased beside her and buried his face in her silky hair, the last thing he heard was a sweetly murmured "Jesse."

Chapter Seven

It was still dark when Alex woke, the heaviness of JJ's arm creating an alien sensation as it lay across her stomach. She felt secure and completely relaxed, something she'd never been able to take pleasure from with Darryl. Her late husband hadn't been considerate of her needs during sex, and always afterward, she'd experienced the feeling of being used.

She'd never known that a lover could be so thoughtful, so in tune with her desires as JJ had been. Not for a second had she perceived that he was dissatisfied or that he found her lacking in any way. In fact, it was because he showed openly just how much he wanted her that she'd felt so uninhibited in their lovemaking. The old urge to cover her nakedness after it was over hadn't surfaced, and she was reluctant to leave the comfort of her lover's embrace.

JJ stirred, his hair-roughened thigh sliding between hers. They seemed to fit together naturally, as if each of their bodies had been made for the other. Alex figured that was just fanciful thinking, given their difference in size.

"What time is it?" he asked in a gravelly tone.

"Three. I should get home soon."

"Worried what your parents might think?" He kissed her collarbone, then her chin.

"They're pretty old-fashioned. What are you doing?"

"Mmm. You have a tiny mole . . . right . . . on . . . this hip."

"That isn't my hip," she gasped.

"There's another on the inner part of your thigh."

"That's not my — stop that!"

He laughed slyly whilst he lifted a leg and braced it on his shoulder, allowing him better access. His tongue tormented her with scorching caresses, driving inside when she begged for release.

Poised on the brink of climax, she grabbed his hair and dragged him up, shoving his big body back on the bed and mounting him swiftly. She rode him hard and fast, a powerful sense of satisfaction rushing through her veins when he tossed his head against the pillow and surged upward, spilling himself mindlessly within her.

Alex collapsed on him as the last ripples of pleasure receded, distantly registering the tenderness with which he rolled them to one side and snuggled close to her still quivering body, a gentle hand feathering damp tendrils of hair away from her face.

"Are you all right?" JJ whispered.

"Never better."

"Never?"

"Nope."

A soft chuckle fanned her lips, and she smiled.

"Sleep for a while longer, baby," he said, "then I'll take you home."

It was nearly five when they eventually succeeded in taking a shower and putting their discarded apparel back on. JJ threw her ruined underwear in the clothes hamper, vowing to have them repaired. He let the filmy material of her slip drift through his fingers musingly, but she snatched it away and shimmied it down over her hips.

The neighborhood was dark and dormant when the car turned onto her parents' street. Most houses had left the porch lights on, and a few still had the traditional red and green lights glowing, but there were no obvious signs of life at that hour.

"I keep forgetting it's only two weeks before Christmas." Alex scrutinized the front of the Eldrich's tiny house when JJ pulled in and shut off the ignition. "I think I'll get out our decorations tomorrow and do something with the yard."

"Don't you mean *today*?"

"Oh, yeah." She blushed.

"Do you mind if I come by later?" His quietly voiced enquiry was tinged with uncertainty. "I'd like to take the boys out for a little while, if that's okay?"

"Sure. If you dare." She tried to gauge his expression, but he seemed to find something very interesting in the pocket of his overcoat and busied himself with rearranging it. "You don't need to spend time with Hank and Billy just because we—"

"I like them," JJ cut her off. "And I happen to like their mother, but don't worry that I'll overstep the boundaries of our . . . ah . . . relationship. No strings, Alex."

She sighed a little forlornly. "They've already got a bad case of hero worship for you, but I think you're good for them. I just don't want them getting any ideas about us."

He gave her a slow nod and a lopsided grin. "Not exactly *Daddy* material, am I?"

"I wouldn't say that. You pay more attention to them than—" She stopped. The comparison she'd been on the verge of making held a ring of disloyalty to Darryl. He'd been a hard worker in the beginning of their marriage and then he'd become terminally ill. She didn't feel right blaming him for his blasé attitude toward the boys. "Hank and Billy just aren't used to having a stable male figure in their lives— besides my father, I mean."

"Stable, huh?"

"Well, you are. No one would guess after seeing you with my sons that you grew up in foster care, JJ. You have a nurturing instinct—"

He gave a shout of laughter.

"You do!" she asserted. "You're going to make a great parent some day for some lucky kids. It'd be a real shame if it didn't happen."

For a long minute, he stared at her. "You honestly believe that, don't you?"

"It's not a stretch."

"While we're on this topic, I feel obligated to point out that the last time we made love, we neglected to use any birth control."

"I'm sorry. That was my fault." *I was too eager to get you where I wanted you.* "It's the wrong time, anyway."

"You ought to apologize," he haughtily informed her. "How shameless you were to take advantage of my vulnerable bod like that! I've never been ravished so thoroughly in my life."

Alex laughed at him. Then, unexpectedly, she yawned.

"See? You've expended all your energy." JJ sobered and leaned over to kiss her gently. "I'd want to know, Alex, if our carelessness led to anything. You wouldn't have to deal with it alone."

"I'm fairly certain I can't get pregnant this time of the month, but if it'll make you feel better I can buy a home test kit in a few days just to make sure," she promised in a soft voice.

"Okay. I'll come by around one for the kids." He kissed her lingeringly once more and waited for her to be safely inside the house before driving off.

"Boy are you taking your chances." That was what Alex had said to him a scant thirty minutes ago when he'd arrived to collect the boys. Now, as he got hauled around a crowded shopping mall by two charging bulls disguised as bundled up, pint-sized children, he recognized the truth in her dire prediction.

After returning to his apartment that morning, he'd tossed and turned on sheets that still held the scent of her and sex. His mind had revisited the details of the hours before, and he'd relinquished his paltry hold on oblivion to doze fitfully while the sounds and images of their lovemaking bombarded his mushy brain.

Presently, the diminutive freight trains were destroying what scrap of sense he still clung to, their curious questions and sporadic attention whittling away the bit of strength he'd restored in those few precious hours of sleep. Even Hank, whom he'd considered sedate during his previous visits to the Eldrich home, had perked up considerably at the prospect of seeing Jolly Old Saint Nick.

"Look, JJ, there's Santa!" Billy's loud cry drew the smiling glances of fellow shoppers. "Can we go sit on his lap?"

"Sure. Just get in line," he instructed, voice calm. His relief at having them distracted was short-lived when he heard Billy's requests.

"A fire engine."

"Yes," Santa responded expectantly, his sharp blue eyes sparkling.

"And a race car."

"Mmm-hmm."

"Aaaand a dad." Billy shot a look at his brother, and Hank dipped his head in surprising agreement.

"A dad with a jeep," clarified the older cohort.

"And he's gotta be real nice to our mom." Billy was apparently just getting warmed up. "And he's gotta read us stories and play Snakes 'n' Ladders wiff us."

JJ passed a hand over his face, recalling the night he'd lost three games to them before Alex had coaxed them off to bed.

Hank leaned against the man garbed in red and white and

seriously chimed in, "If he doesn't have any kids, that's all right 'cause him and Mom'll make some more."

The group of onlookers who'd become enthralled with the innocent conversation hee-hawed in merriment and some even applauded.

JJ groaned. The boys already had *ideas* about he and Alex. This could be problematic, he surmised. Knowing he had no business encouraging it, for Alex would be incensed, he decided not to sour the mood with grave warnings that their plans would not bear fruit.

Four hours later, he flopped onto the couch next to George Eldrich and tiredly remarked, "I am in awe of you. How do you keep track of them in a ball park?"

"I find a seat in the well-traveled path of a vendor," he replied, never taking his gaze from the TV. "As long as they can sniff the hot dogs, they're pretty docile."

JJ was invited to help string the outdoor lights along the eaves of the house and was at a loss momentarily as he vacillated between making tracks and letting on how completely inept he was with holiday paraphernalia.

"I've never strung lights before," he explained to Alex, apologetic. "I'll need direction."

"Climb up on the ladder, and I'll pass them to you. Staple the wire to the wood."

So, taking his life in his hands, he positioned himself gingerly on the top rung and tacked on three bulbs successfully. Alex whistled at his accomplishment—and the favorable view of his butt. Bulb number four joined the others, and he had to extend his arms cautiously to avoid losing his precarious balance. When he took his hand away, the glove he was wearing stayed where it was, dangling by the thumb piece.

"Uh, you probably shouldn't staple your clothing up there. The neighbors will complain."

Alex's lips trembled visibly.

"I did that deliberately," JJ fibbed. "You can tell everyone it belongs to Santa."

She nodded. "Good idea."

"I thought so."

Darkness was falling when they went inside, the tantalizing smell of gingerbread wafting around them. His mouth watered as the distinct aroma nudged a memory of one of his foster mothers. Addy had been his favorite, the only guardian who'd taken the time to make Christmas truly special for him. She'd enticed him into sticking his little nine-year-old hands in her doughy concoctions and sat with him in her big kitchen for hours, looking over his bony shoulder while he'd cut slices of gingerbread to go in the oven. Addy's was the only face that he could still recall with vivid detail, her hazel eyes brimming with laughter, cherubic cheeks pink from the heat of the kitchen.

"JJ?" Alex tugged on his coat sleeve. "Mom was wondering if you'd stay for dinner."

"Sure." He shook himself mentally and removed his outer clothing.

"Everything all right? You were a mile away a minute ago."

The tiny kitchen was spilling over with pies and cookies when he stepped in behind her. "Oh, no. It's just that smell." He gestured to the counter and dropped his chilled bones into a chair. "It reminds me of a lady who took care of me once. It was a tradition for her to make this big gingerbread house every Christmas. The year I was there, she let me help." He folded his hands on the tabletop and stared at them, idly twirling his thumbs when he remembered the kind woman.

"What was her name?" Alex took the seat across from him.

"Adeline Martin—Addy. I wasn't with her long."

"You liked her."

He flicked her a glance, and the tips of his ears burned. Shrugging casually, he said, "Yeah."

"Where is she now?"

"I'm not sure. She had to relocate to the Burin peninsula—Lawn, I think—to take care of a sister who was ill. Of course, I couldn't go with her." He sipped from the mug she'd set before him. "What's this, hot toddy?"

"Mom goes all out for Christmas," she wryly answered. "Hot toddy, fruit cakes, the works."

"It's got a kick to it."

"Mmm-hmm." She paused and then cleared her throat. "So, did you ever try to find her?"

"Who?"

"Addy."

Surprised, he queried, "Why would I?"

"Well, she seems to have stuck in your mind. Don't you ever wonder what happened to her?"

JJ lifted his shoulders and said nothing.

"Maybe she wonders about you, too."

"I doubt it, Alex. Foster parents don't tend to get attached. Not the ones I had, anyway. Addy was one of the better ones. That's why I remember her so well." He'd never mentioned his former foster mother to anyone, not even Nance, whom he'd met shortly after. The thought made him uneasy, so he changed the subject.

Alex stood in the bedroom doorway and surveyed the picture before her. The boys had pleaded for JJ to read them a story, and he'd willingly agreed, letting them drag him off for what had become a nightly ritual. But instead of coming back to the living room to talk for a while, he'd apparently fallen asleep along with his fans. His blond head lay nestled on Hank's pillow, his face as innocent as the other two rising and falling with every breath that expanded his wide chest, each of his tightly muscled arms curved protectively around a pajama-clad little boy as they cuddled into him trustingly.

A lump formed in her throat at the sight of those dark heads next to JJ's lighter one, and she moved forward, stooping down to pick up the book that had come to rest on his flat stomach. His arms tensed reflexively like he'd sensed another presence in his sleep, the motion making her think he was safeguarding his charges by instinct.

"JJ," she whispered.

Bleary-eyed, he grinned. "I knew you were an angel."

"Funny. Help me get these two settled." They carefully moved Billy to the twin bed next to his brother's and tucked them both in. Alex turned out the light and left the door ajar so the illumination from the hallway would reassure the boys if they should wake in the middle of the night.

They crept out to the living room, JJ yawning hugely on the way.

"I'll get some sheets and blankets for the couch," she began, but he shook his head.

"That isn't necessary. I'm fine." He smothered another yawn.

"You're zonked. You can't drive home."

"I won't fit on that thing lying down."

"It unfolds."

JJ eyed it, dubious.

"Really," she maintained. "It's very comfortable."

"Aren't you sick of seeing my mug?"

"Not particularly. You wear it well."

He ambled closer. "Kiss me, and I'll think about it."

Mindful of her parents sleeping in the other room, she reached up and pecked him on the cheek.

"You can't want me to stay very badly, Alex. That was

pitiful."

She sighed and brushed her mouth across his. "Better?"

"Mmmmm." He waggled his head from side to side in contemplation. "Not much."

Grabbing him by the ears, she traced her tongue along his lower lip and sucked on it slowly, tenderly nipping at his mouth. He wrapped his arms around her and hoisted her up until she was level with him. She obliged him by taking the hint and planting her lips eagerly on his, kissing him deeply and at a leisurely pace while she slipped her hands through his curly hair to massage his scalp.

"How's that?" Alex murmured against his mouth.

"Perfect."

"Now let me get some blankets."

JJ hugged her tightly and let her slide down his obviously excited body. "All right, but I'll make the bed. You don't need to wait on me."

"Whatever makes you happy."

"Since your family is sleeping next door, I can't show you what would *really* make me happy."

"Lecher," she accused and went to retrieve the bed linens.

"I'm an honorable sort," he argued. "I would never throw myself at you if you didn't invite me to."

Alex snickered indelicately. "I saw what you had in your pocket."

"But I restrained myself admirably."

Once the bed was straightened out, he began to strip. Alex watched him openly, ignoring his arched eyebrow when he pretended to *discover* she hadn't left the room. Bare-chested and wearing only his white briefs, he scuttled beneath the covers and lay back with his hands behind his head.

"Turn the light out as you leave, you hussy."

"Yes, sweetums," she replied tamely.

"Alex?"

"Hmm?"

"You really didn't mind that I stayed this evening?" Heavy lids drooped over his blue eyes, obscuring their expression.

"I'm glad you're here," she told him honestly and flipped off the light. She'd become alarmingly fond of having him around, but there wasn't a lot she could do about it. *He just grows on you, doesn't he?* a little voice piped up in her head. *Yeah,* she responded, *he certainly does.* "Goodnight, Alex."

"Goodnight . . . Jesse," she whispered.

Monday morning came, and JJ tapped his fingers on the steering wheel as he waited for Alex to emerge from the house. He felt carefree and lighthearted after spending the weekend with the Eldrich family—he was enchanted with the boys and had developed a healthy respect for the older couple who'd raised Alex.

That he was nuts about the woman was a given, but he chose not to examine those feelings too closely, instead pledging to take it one step at a time so as not to frighten her away from the intimacy they'd shared these last few days. She'd said she didn't want a relationship, and he believed she thought she meant it. The thing was, he recognized that they'd already begun something special, and it was a revelation to him—he'd never imagined that he could care for another person so quickly and as deeply as he did for Alex, hadn't thought he was capable of it. But he'd shocked himself with the intensity of his emotions, and after a night of soul searching, had decided that it felt pretty damned good.

He was still having a bit of difficulty with the fact that he'd been so brainless as to forget protection while making love to her. Even as a randy teenager, he'd been adamant about using condoms. Maybe there was a tiny part of him that longed to see Alex nursing an infant with blond hair, but it was selfish and downright foolhardy to want to burden her with that responsibility at this point in her life.

The object of his pondering exited the house and ran down the walk to his jeep, stuffing a crust of toast in her mouth.

"Sorry," she mumbled, "I slept in."

"No rush. You left your hair down."

"Too unprofessional? I didn't have time to braid it."

He leaned over and buried his face in the fragrant, silky mane. Then, after some consideration, he wrapped the raven tresses around his wrists.

"What are you up to now?" Laughter shone from her brown eyes.

"I figured if I gave in to the urge to do this before we get to the office, I can stay focused for the rest of the day."

"I'll fix it when we get there."

"No, leave it." He kissed her. "I'd best get that out of the way, too."

"Uh-huh. No touching at work," she commanded.

"Oh, Alex," he sighed heavily.

"Oh, Jesse."

"Oh God."

"Just drive."

The day zipped by, interspersed with flirting glances and suggestive leers—*his*—and smothered giggles coupled with wry shakes of the head—*hers*.

JJ loved seeing her so happy and wondered if he'd contributed to the bounce in her step or if it was simply that life in general was on the upswing. Ultimately, he didn't care what the reasons were. Whatever kept the glow on her sweet face was fine with him, whether he could be credited with a part of it or not.

Just as that thought formed in his mind, he glimpsed a rather nondescript man approaching Alex's desk. He froze, a shred of recognition surfacing as he watched the scene through the open door of his office. Several times, he'd run into the guy at the courthouse, and he struggled to recall what his job was. Then it hit him — *hard*.

"Alexandra Manning?"

Squinting up from the spreadsheet on the computer screen, Alex frowned at the use of her given name. No one bothered using it unless it was for something medical or very official.

"I was told I could find Alexandra Manning in here?" The plain man prodded her smilingly.

"I'm Alex."

He reached inside his coat and withdrew an ivory-colored envelope. Placing it squarely in front of her, he announced, "You have been served. Good day." And with that, he left.

A horrible coldness invaded her as she stared fixedly at the fiendish envelope. She knew exactly what was inside without having to look. *Damn them!* With shaking hands, she extracted the document and perused it quickly, her vision blurring as it landed on the dreaded phrase *petition for sole guardianship*. The thick papers fluttered to the desk unheeded, and she covered her face with shaking hands.

Someone grasped her quaking shoulders and, try as she might, she could not comprehend the words she knew were being spoken over her head. Her chair was pulled back, and she felt distanced while her useless brain endeavored to catch up.

"Here, sit down." The commanding tone finally got her attention. "Nance?" JJ yelled. "Could you bring Alex some water?" He pushed her into a chair and chafed her limp hands between his. "You're shivering, Alex. What was that all about? Isn't that guy a process server or something?"

Nance materialized and thrust a glass before her. JJ helped her sip from it, taking care not to slosh the liquid all over the carpet and themselves. She turned her head away, motioning that she'd had enough.

"They're suing for full custody," she mumbled crossly.

"Elizabeth and what's-his-face?"

"Gerard."

"Whatever," JJ groused. "The stuck-up paragons of right-eousness are suing you for custody?"

She nodded dumbly as tears welled up and spilled over, coursing hotly down her cheeks. "On the grounds that I'm an unfit parent who can't provide for my sons' welfare."

"Oh, honey," tutted Nance sympathetically, "that'll never fly in court." She handed Alex a wad of tissues and patted her shoulder.

"She's right." JJ took the tissues and blotted her face with care. "A stand-up bunch of character witnesses will shoot down such a ludicrous charge."

"You don't understand. I can't afford a decent lawyer, and they'll drag this out as long as possible."

"They can't have unlimited funds themselves, Alex. You said the Mannings weren't as well off as —"

"Elizabeth's brother is an attorney. A good one." She closed her eyes and let a shuddering breath escape. "It won't be long before he starts making noise about how I've been unemployed for a long period of time, that I've had to go on public assistance, et cetera."

Nance said, "Everyone falls on hard times now and then. You're working now, too."

Alex grimaced. "Two weeks at a new job won't sound like much to a judge."

"I'll pay for a lawyer —"

"No, JJ."

"Alex—"

"*No!* That'll just be one more debt I can't repay."

"I wouldn't expect you to right away." He stood and paced in front of the window animatedly.

"Forget it. And don't suggest it again, please." The thought of her new lover giving her money for anything, no matter how important, had her skin crawling. "I'll go to Legal Aid."

Nance excused herself when someone came into the other office and closed the door behind her. The sudden silence was broken only by the scuff of JJ's shoes while he walked around aimlessly.

"I don't put much faith in those lawyers, Alex. They're too green."

"I'll figure something out. It isn't your problem."

"Hell it isn't!" he grumbled. "I care about you, and you needn't think I'll stand by and watch those snobs railroad you. Being stubborn about it won't help, so get over it."

"Yes, boss." Some of her equilibrium had been restored just listening to his staunch defense of her mothering skills, but his unyielding support had boosted her confidence even more.

"Don't call me that."

"Well, you are . . . *sir.*"

He sat on the edge of his desk and faced her. "I hope I'm also your friend."

"It's a little hard to think of you in that context after . . . well, you know."

"You must be referring to that mind-blowing night this past weekend when you had your wicked way with me." Blond eyebrows bounced up and down.

Alex almost smiled. "You didn't object."

"No, I didn't, did I?" He took her hands, drawing her out

of her seat and into his embrace. She went willingly and rested her forehead against his. "It's quittin' time, ma'am," he drawled in an atrocious southern accent. "What say we mosey outta here?"

"Okay." Leaning in for a hug, she told him, "I really needed this. I feel much better."

"Try not to worry about that stupid custody suit. We'll figure something out."

She nodded and left in search of her coat.

All that evening and into the wee hours of the morning, the looming threat of a court battle nagged at her. She didn't tell her parents about it, keeping the legal document out of sight in her purse. They certainly didn't need the added stress after all they'd done for her these last couple of years, and she was determined to stand on her own. But that resolution was shaky at best, and it would only take a minor knock to cause it to crumble.

The knock was more like a *whack* when it came early the following morning, all the more powerful for its sudden arrival.

There on her parents' doorstep was a composed, straight-faced, blond Adonis with what he claimed was the ideal solution to her problems. Braced for an outlandish scheme of some sort, she nonetheless nearly fainted when JJ Vanzant uttered the most extraordinary phrase to ever come out of his beautifully sculpted mouth.

"Marry me."

CHAPTER EIGHT

The next day, JJ was still trying to convince her that his proposal was the ideal solution. He'd very matter-of-factly made his argument, ticking off the pros of their getting married on his fingers while she steadfastly ignored him. His methods of persuasion were exhausted, so he settled now for systematically wearing down her resistance with sheer obstinacy. He'd spent the twenty-something hours since devising his little plot in the darkness of his bedroom going over and over the benefits a marriage of convenience had to offer. Alex wouldn't have to worry about money, the kids would have a comfortable home and two loving parents instead of one, the Mannings wouldn't stand a chance in hell of being awarded custody in the face of this new development, and the arrangement had the unmistakable appeal of a fabulous affair between consenting adults for as long as it took for the sexual sparks to die a natural death. Or at least, that was what he claimed in the hopes that he could convince himself of it, as well.

"Alex, could you come in here a moment?" He disconnected the intercom and waited for her to stomp into his office. She'd been doing that all day, ever since he'd had the *unmitigated nerve* to suggest an evening at his place where they could discuss the merits of holy matrimony in peace.

Grimly, JJ reflected that it was not even a month ago that he'd jokingly ridiculed his friend for tying the knot, and now, here he was, doing his damnedest to drag a reluctant female to the altar himself. And he'd already begun using those mushy phrases like *sweetheart*, *darling*, and *baby*, words he'd never dared utter to a woman before Alex. In fact, he'd been spouting the endearments for weeks, inserting them into conversations with her as if it were an everyday occurrence.

"What is it now?" The door banged shut behind her, and she stood, feet braced apart, glaring mutinously at him.

It was a touch intimidating that she was being so obtuse about marrying him. He wasn't *that* bad a catch, was he?

"I just wanted to thank you for the diligence with which you've rearranged my filing system," JJ properly stated. "Everyone is raving about it."

She blinked. "My diligence?"

"The filing system."

"Oh." She frowned prettily at the compliment. "But you didn't want me to do it."

"I'm flexible." Busying his twitching hands with something in the desk drawer, he feigned disinterest when he probed, "So, are you ready to discuss my proposal?"

"No. Is that all?"

He flung the drawer closed and pinned her with his determined gaze. "No. You haven't been listening."

"I have and I think marriage is a rotten idea."

"Rotten for us or just in general?"

"For us." Turning for the door, she added, "I don't want to be at the mercy of another person when it comes to finances or anything else. That's exactly what would happen."

JJ leaped from his seat and prevented her from making a hasty exit. He directed her to his vacant chair and propped her in it. "I don't want to trap you, Alex. I believe we can agree on the details of the arrangement before we take our vows and avoid any messiness later on. If you like, I'll have a prenuptial document drawn up to protect you from being abandoned either physically or financially. I'm not playing a game here."

"Do you hear yourself? *Arrangement* is not exactly the word most commonly used when referring to marriage."

"I'm well aware that your affections are otherwise engaged and I really don't expect that you'll suddenly fall in love with me—"

"What's this about my affections?" she stridently demanded. "I'm not seeing anyone."

"You're seeing me."

"You know what I meant."

"Yes," he snapped, pacing the carpet. "But I was talking about Darryl. Don't deny it," he said when she seemed ready to object. "If you weren't still carrying a torch for your husband, you wouldn't have such a problem with marrying me."

"My reasons for not wanting to get married are as simple as I said they were. I don't want to have to depend on anyone—period!"

"Because he died and left you alone and it tore you apart," he finished doggedly.

"There's more to it than that."

"So, enlighten me."

She spat, "It's none of your bloody business."

"Oh, isn't it?" JJ bent down and shoved a hand through her hair, anchoring her head for his kiss. Astonished that he was so riled at the idea of her being stuck on her dead mate, he let the pent-up hostility show, uncaring if he came across as resentful. Because he did resent Darryl Manning, the phantom perfect husband from her past, and for that unguarded moment, he wanted her to know it.

A helpless moan cut through the red haze enveloping his brain, and he gentled the kiss, gradually easing the pressure as shame pummeled his conscience. He loosened his hold, a sigh escaping as he knelt before her.

"I'm sorry." He pressed his forehead to hers and touched the swollen line of her bottom lip. "You ought to slap me again for acting like an ogre."

"I'm tempted." But instead, she placed warm hands against his cheeks and dipped her head to taste him delicately, angling closer when he surrendered control of the embrace and just savored the sweet caress.

For a long time, she sipped at his mouth and stroked the tense set of his shoulders, easing the pressure he'd let build inside him. She traced the edge of his teeth with her tongue and swallowed the barely audible groan that rose from his throat. When she lifted her head, he stared fuzzily into her dark eyes and concentrated on breathing.

"Well," he said thickly, "I certainly didn't deserve that."

Alex grinned. "I did."

Exhaling loudly, he attempted one final assault on her stubborn resistance. "Just give me five minutes to make my case without interruption, and I won't bring up the topic of marriage again."

"JJ, it'd be a big mistake for us to—"

"Three minutes."

"Fine," she huffed. "Three minutes. You're on the clock, mister."

"First of all," he resolutely began, "I can't pretend that I know a heck of a lot about raising kids or being part of a family unit, but I'm fond of Hank and Billy and I promise to be there for them and you for as long as I'm needed. I want to share in the responsibility of caring for them, Alex, not just come to work and go home claiming my job as parent stops with economic concerns. I want to take the boys to ball games and help tuck them in at night.

"Secondly, I don't expect you to quit working if that's what you want. Although, I was thinking that you might want to finish that degree you once dreamed of and try your hand at teaching. I'll support you in your career choice and do my best to make it possible for you." He conveyed the sincerity of this last statement with a level look, imparting his wholehearted endorsement of her goals. Alex deserved to be who she wanted on her own terms, and he knew she'd make a wonderful teacher.

"Furthermore, while I had suggested this as a temporary arrangement, I would like you to keep an open mind about the long haul. I'm discovering that I do have a nesting instinct, after all, and I hope you'll consider the possibility of us giving Hank and Billy a sibling or two — not right away — maybe in a year or two? That's providing, of course, the deed hasn't been done already." JJ ended his shortened speech breathlessly. "Is my time up?"

"Pretty much. I'm not pregnant, by the way. I took a test *and* I'm taking the pill now."

Her eyes had grown wide at the mention of more children, and he realized that he'd shocked her. Hell, he'd shocked himself. But the more he thought about it, the more he liked the idea of expanding their family. If Alex agreed, that was.

"You can tell with one of those little home jobbies so soon?" When she nodded, he buried the pang of disappointment that had flared in his chest. "Will you at least think about what I've said? Seriously?" He stood and pulled her up after him. "We have something special, Alex. I'm not sure what it is, but it's nothing I've come across before. I'd like to have the chance to explore it."

She bowed her head a bit. "I'll think it over, but I honestly don't know if — I'll think it over," she promised loudly when he uttered a pained sound.

"Thank you. If you want to ask me anything, I'll be at home all evening with Jonas and Steven. They're going to pick my brain about a surveillance program they want to design." JJ gave her a careful hug, still feeling a bit guilty for his roughness earlier. The scent of her silky hair tickled his senses, and he mumbled, "I still want you, no matter what you decide. It seems like ages since we—"

"I know." Alex chuckled. "Even with all that's going on, I can't get the other night out of my head. I still want you, too."

"I think we'll have to make another date soon. I need some . . . sustenance."

He released her and grabbed his coat. "Now, I'm going to take you home and let you ponder my proposal. Call me?"

She replied with a soft, "I will."

The dirty rat!

The next day, Alex hefted the file in her hand and cringed. There amongst the pile she'd bumped off his desk was a thin folder with her name on it.

Feeling faint, she grappled for a chair and almost fell into it. She focused on the date in the right-hand corner as her shaking hands fluttered over it.

We have something special, Alex . . .

Horse pucky, you rogue.

Thinking she'd tidy up his desk and make sure no wayward files had been missed for her catalogue, she'd pulled a stack out of the drawer and laid them on the corner. Her heart had stopped and then shrank a little when her own name had jumped out to greet her after they'd fallen.

A chill crept into her body as she realized he'd had the thing for weeks, all the while asking those concerned questions about her life, her marriage . . . *he knew!*

"What are you doing?"

She looked up to find JJ standing in the doorway, still as stone. His eyes were hard as glass until he saw what she held. Then, guilt flooded them.

"My job," she replied woodenly and threw the file at his feet. "I see you've been doing yours."

"Alex—"

"Do you do this to everyone you meet or just the women who turn you down?" Anger took hold, and she flared, "What happened to our being *friends?*"

"I never opened the damn thing, I promise you. I shoved it in the drawer and left it." His fervent statement seemed legitimate, but she'd been fooled by a man once.

"How can you propose marriage for any reason and expect me to trust you after you've been invading my privacy, digging up old personal business?"

He rubbed a hand across his forehead and puffed out a breath. "That's not how it was. Hell, that's a lie. I had it for the sole purpose of figuring you out. I can't explain why, but I didn't look at it, Alex."

In a dull tone she asked, "Why should I believe that?"

JJ let his head fall back and stared at the ceiling. "The truth is simply that it felt like it was underhanded and intrusive—there's no justification for my doing it. Professional hazard, maybe."

Wanting badly to have some faith in him, she calmly sought reassurance. "You really didn't look at it?"

"I swear on my life—Nance's life," he affirmed. His countenance was so steady, his eyes so plainly vulnerable, that she couldn't believe he was lying.

"All right." She stood. "But I don't want a repeat of this, JJ, not if you want me to contemplate . . . you know."

"I know." He sighed. "I'm sorry. Your business is your own unless you decide to share it."

Alex nodded. "What did you come back for, anyway?"

He gave her a gentle kiss on the cheek. "Just to tell you that I hope you earnestly consider . . . you know."

She smiled a fraction. "I know."

"Do you intend to split the housework?" Alex demanded of him hours later. The phone was wedged between her chin and her shoulder as she smoothed icing on a layer of chocolate cake.

"Certainly. I can pick up my own underwear and do laundry. I do have one habit that I'm told is rather annoying, but I've managed to keep the apartment relatively clean."

"Habit?"

"Hmm. Jonas says it's bad manners to put the milk carton back in the fridge. After it's empty, I mean."

"Yeah, you'll have to stop that." She hung up. Two minutes later, she dialed again. "Are we going to live in your apartment?"

"It's too small for the four of us. There's a house fairly close to the Mackenzie estate I've been looking at. It's big, and there's tons of yard space. You know the area."

"Mmm-hmm." Licking icing from her pinky, she remarked, "Very nice," and cradled the receiver again.

Lorna stepped into the kitchen and, seeing the mess, retreated to the living room to watch TV with her husband. The boys were firmly ensconced in their room for the night, having exhausted themselves making snowmen next door.

Alex mulled over the concept of sharing a home with JJ as she poured a cup of coffee and plunked down at the table. She still could not digest the fact that he was serious in his efforts to get her to tie the knot. He was really offering her the opportunity to change her life and the lives of her children. But how much stock could she put in his promises? Hadn't she learned not to trust so completely in her first marriage?

JJ isn't Darryl, her inner voice reminded her. That was true. She had seen no evidence that he'd go back on his word to anyone. But how did he feel about honouring his wedding vows? A lot of people these days didn't bat an eyelash at having flings.

He answered after the first ring. "I'd insist on absolute fidelity. I *cannot* abide cheating."

"I have no intention of carrying on behind your back. I'm monogamous. I swear to be faithful." JJ's voice dropped to a whisper. "And why the hell would I want anyone else? You wear me out as it is."

She hung up.

There was no reason for her to refuse, was there? He'd eliminated every single question she had. As long as he stuck to his word once they were married, she couldn't think of a valid objection.

It wasn't as if she hadn't been tempted from the moment he'd suggested the holy union—after all, he was successful, well-off financially, sexy, sweet, funny. Infuriating sometimes. Stubborn, too, but not unreasonably so. The boys adored him, and he obviously cared for them a great deal.

Who was she kidding? Alex was half in love with the man already.

"Yes?" He sounded vaguely amused when next she called.

"Am I bothering you?"

"No. I'm glad you're taking me seriously. What's your question?"

"Well, I was wondering . . . if you intended to adopt Hank and Billy. Not that it's a requirement or anything."

"Yes. If it's okay with them." Was it her imagination, or did his response have a slight tremor to it?

"I believe they're partial to you."

"Are you?" he quietly prompted.

"Definitely. I'll call you back."

The dial tone buzzed in his ear, and he grinned. Alex's opposition was weakening. The fact that she'd asked about him adopting the boys was a good sign, and it had touched him deeply. The idea of being entrusted with her sons wasn't nearly as daunting as it would have been months ago. He found himself looking forward to it.

"See that," tsked Steven pitifully from his seat on the couch. "He's a goner. I knew it was contagious."

"Maybe you should leave, Kincaid." Jonas tossed his notepad down on the coffee table. "It might rub off."

"I am immune."

"Sure."

"I am. Isn't that goofy face he's wearing a bit frightening?" Steven peered closely at JJ and shook his head mournfully. "Man, he's sunk."

The redhead grunted ruefully. "Worse things could happen."

"I'm not falling for that. Are you okay, Vanzant?"

"Mmm-hmm. Dandy. Are you two finished grilling me or what? Did you get all the information you needed?"

Steven quirked an eyebrow. "We got no information. Zip. Nada. You're useless."

"We'll try another time," Jonas said sympathetically, seemingly identifying completely with the workings of an infatuated mind.

"Yeah. I'm outta here, too." Steven wiped imaginary tears from his eyes and plaintively whined, "Soon, I'll be the only man left standing."

"Get out, Stevie. Your time will come." JJ saw them to the door amid more good-natured ribbing.

The phone whirred just as he returned to his arm chair. "Hello, Alex."

"How did you know it was me?"

"Lucky guess," he dryly intoned.

She laughed huskily, the sexy sound dancing along his nerves and straight to his lower anatomy. "I've come to a decision."

"And?" His grip on the receiver was ferocious as his entire being tensed up. The moment of truth was upon him. Would she think he was good enough for her? Did he really believe he was worthy of the chance to have a family, a life with her? Could he be blessed with the gift of lying next to her every night and waking up to her every morning?

"Yes."

The single syllable reverberated through his soul, releasing a pool of emotion that swelled his heart and set it pounding at a joyous pace. He hadn't known there was actually such a thing as euphoria until it hit him with dizzying force.

"Are you sure, Alex?" He managed to sound quite normal, as if he received an answer to a marriage proposal every day.

"I'm sure."

JJ swallowed the lump in his throat. "You won't regret it."

"I'll see you in the morning. Bye."

"Bye," he replied, still stunned, and hung up. For a long time, he sat and sightlessly stared at the opposite wall. Then he vaulted from his chair and howled at the top of his lungs. *Alex is going to marry me!*

The phone cut into his gleeful racket, and he examined the contraption with some trepidation. Had she changed her mind? Had she recognized in those scant seconds what a colossal mistake she could be making?

"Hello."

Firmly, Alex pronounced, "There's just one thing I want you to promise me, JJ."

An ominous shiver ran up his spine. "What's that?"

"If you become unhappy in our . . . ah . . . situation, I want you to tell me so that we can proceed with an amicable divorce."

Some of the tension left him. "That won't happen." He was as sure of that as he was of the color of his eyes.

"I know you don't believe in love and happy-ever-afters—I'm not sure that I do, either—but if you should meet someone and you want to be with her, then I don't want you to feel obligated to me and the boys. I want you to be honest with me about it."

"Alex, there will never come a time when I think of you and the boys as an obligation." He thought the idea was laughable but appreciated the concern for his happiness.

"Promise me."

"Sweetheart—"

"JJ!"

"All right, I promise. But it won't happen."

Alex sighed, the exasperated sound echoing in his ear. "This is a big sacrifice for you. You're giving up a bachelor lifestyle to help me keep custody of Hank and Billy. I mean, pardon the triteness of my question, but what's in it for you?"

"You," he truthfully confessed. "Plus, two great kids for whom I also have an unwavering affection. I wouldn't call spending my life with you a sacrifice, darling." The roughness of his tone said plainly that he was contemplating the intimate aspect of their relationship.

"I think you mean your bed."

"That, too. Especially that."

"Uh-huh. So, when will we have the wedding?"

"New Year's Eve," JJ declared, liking the sentimental notion of beginning their lives together as husband and wife on a new calendar.

"*New Year's Eve?* I take it you don't want a big to-do? Just friends and family?"

He hesitated. "If you'd prefer a large ceremony—"

"No, I like the idea of a small wedding. It seems more . . . um . . . intimate?" She sounded faintly embarrassed to be using the term, and he grinned.

"I like intimate."

"I just didn't think you'd be in a hurry. The thirty-first is less than two weeks away."

"Well," he mumbled, casting about for an excuse to hide his eagerness, "the sooner we say *I do*, the sooner Elizabeth and Gerard will take a hike."

"Yeah, I guess you're right." A smothered yawn reached across the line.

"Get some sleep. Tomorrow, we're going house-hunting. Nance and the guys can cover at the office. I'll pick you up around nine."

"Okay. G'night."

"Goodnight, Alex," JJ murmured, already anticipating the day ahead.

Hank and Billy were sleeping soundly when she padded quietly into their room. Carefully tugging the blankets around each of her sons more securely, Alex told herself she was doing the right thing. They needed a father, and she honestly couldn't imagine a better man for the position than the one she'd just agreed to marry. She'd noticed that in the short time they'd known JJ, the boys had developed a strong inclination to bond with him, automatically trusting and welcoming his presence. He'd yet to acknowledge his significance, but she believed that eventually he would realize the profound depth of fondness and devotion they felt for him.

Tiptoeing out to the living room, she leaned against the doorjamb and announced to her parents, "JJ and I are getting married on New Year's Eve."

Lorna's ecstatic "How wonderful, dear!" clashed with

George's "Good God, Alex, you're not pregnant?"

She spent twenty minutes trying to lower her father's blood pressure and another ten mopping up her mother's delighted tears. By the time she crawled under the covers, she was worn out. In the split second before slipping into unconsciousness, the thought struck her that soon she would be sharing her bed and everything else with a certain sexy private investigator. A smile pulled on her lips as she drifted into sleep.

CHAPTER NINE

"When you told me it was big with lots of yard space, I thought you meant—big with lots of yard space." Alex gaped at the size of the split-level house. The rambling structure sat atop a sloping lawn, its windows gleaming in the morning sun. It reminded her of a picture she'd once seen in a magazine of a Spanish hacienda, except the trees and bushes surrounding it were barren and there were patches of snow everywhere. She imagined that when they bloomed in the spring, it would be a glorious riot of color. The walkway was wide and tiled with red brick, a single step leading to a set of ornately carved wooden doors. The walls had the appearance of white-washed stone, and underneath every lower window was a flower box, loaded now with more white stuff.

Tall firs and pine trees dotted the immense tract of land on which the house stood, seeming to crowd in and protect the building from the harshness of winter and provide much-needed shade for the hot days of summer.

JJ parked the jeep on the circular drive and shut off the ignition. They both sat in silence and gazed at the house.

"How much *yard* is there, exactly?" Alex probed when she found her voice again.

"Just a couple acres." Her new fiancé tapped his fingers on the steering wheel, a frown of concentration marking his features. "There's a pool house adjoining the back, and a garage over on the right." He motioned vaguely.

"A two-car garage?" Her question had a slight squeak to

it.

"Uh . . . three, I think."

"JJ, this place must cost a fortune. I had pictured something a little more . . . ah . . . *little.*"

JJ shrugged, his attention still riveted on the house. "Six bedrooms, two and a half baths, walk-in closets, et cetera. The real estate agent says the kitchen, dining room, and living areas are huge. Oh, and the den," he tacked on. "I believe she said there was a library, too."

"This is a mini mansion."

"Mmm."

"I don't mean to sound rude, but can you afford this?"

He bounced his eyebrows up and down. "Don't worry, Alex. My buddy Stevie is a quirky individual with a knack for making wise investments. A few he's made for me have turned over a nice profit. Besides, I own a successful company. Collateral wouldn't be a problem if I had to get a loan — which I don't, thank God."

Alex forced herself to relax. Memories of Darryl's reckless spending had jumped up to bite her. Again, she kicked herself for comparing JJ to her footloose and negligent late husband.

She really had to stop trying to identify similarities between the two. It was almost as if she expected the same disappointment with JJ, and it was unfair — he'd done nothing but show her just how different from Darryl he was.

"Alex?"

"Hmm?"

"I asked if you wanted to go inside." He dangled a key in front of her. "The agent said she'd be here shortly, but if she got held up to go in and look around."

"They don't normally give the keys to people, do they?" Suspicion had crept into her voice.

JJ laughed slyly. "I was very persuasive."

"I'll bet. The woman probably thinks you'll make a down payment today. You didn't tell her you might, did you?"

"Well, perhaps I came off as being practically, almost, fairly sure that we'd like the place." He grinned, all innocence.

"You've already seen the inside, haven't you?"

"Do you know that your luscious mouth tends to fall open a lot?"

"JJ!" she gritted, poking him in the ribs.

"Ouch! All right, I saw it yesterday." He dimpled dazzlingly.

"You were awfully sure of yourself."

"No, no. I was looking at it for myself. That way, if you turned down my offer of marriage, I could start up an exclusive monastic retreat." JJ's deadpan expression would have been faultless were it not for the glimmer in his blue eyes. "I'd have sworn off women forever."

Alex snickered at that and got out of the jeep. She hunched her shoulders against the cold and waited while he unlocked the solid oak doors. Intuition told her that the interior would be grand and spacious, but her imagination did not do justice to the genuine article.

Hardwood floors had apparently been taken care of by some fastidious soul, Alex noted as she stepped down to the enormous living room. The previous owner's furniture had not left one single mark on the immaculately polished strips of wood. A fireplace dominated the far wall, its mantelpiece just the right width for displaying photographs. A staircase climbed to the upper level. Upon inspection, she discovered that it led to the bedrooms and baths, one of which contained a large shower stall and a hot tub. Hours of lounging in heated waters with her future husband popped into her lascivious brain, and she scurried forward, lest he read her mind.

She passed through an open door and stopped, the sight of the grounds through multi-paned windows stealing her breath. Shelves lined the walls, and she easily summoned an image of how they would look overflowing with books.

Wandering back through the halls, she located the master bedroom. Set apart from the rest and containing its own private bathroom, it also had a panoramic view of the *yard*. She sat on the padded window seat and inhaled deeply.

"The kids would desecrate those beautiful floors." Alex looked back at JJ, who'd silently followed her around and watched her reaction.

"Rugs," he said, as if that explained everything.

"We can't put rugs everywhere. It defeats the purpose of having hardwood flooring."

"Hank and Billy can be careful." At her raised eyebrow, he added, "We can have them refinished when needed." He sat facing her and awaited the next objection.

"It seems pretty far from the city."

JJ patiently informed her, "The Mackenzie estate is five minutes from here, my office is ten, the schools are in between by bus, *and* there are a smattering of specialty shops in the area—a fairly large grocery store included. Personally, I like being on the outskirts of town, it's quieter."

"You've all but made up your mind, haven't you?" She laughed at his sheepish expression.

"If you'd rather keep searching—"

"No. I love it."

He scooped her into his lap and smacked a kiss on her surprised mouth. "Did you see the Jacuzzi? And that humungous shower?" Unzipping her parka, he slipped his big hands beneath her sweater. "Just imagine what we could find to do in there."

Alex shoved the coat from his shoulders and nibbled his neck. "What about the rest of the house?"

"Oh, we could do it all over the house." A groan escaped him, and she found his earlobe and tugged on it gently, scraping her teeth sensuously along his heated skin.

"I mean, I haven't seen it yet."

"I have. You'll love that, too." JJ's breathing had become erratic, his arousal very prominent against her hip. "Come here and kiss me, Alex. I haven't stopped thinking about this for days."

He cupped her breasts and stroked her as his tongue dueled with hers. She adjusted their position so she sat astride him, moaning softly when his erection pressed hard into the apex of her thighs.

"Closer," he urged, fumbling with her jeans. He released the button and dealt with the zipper hastily, working one hand inside the denim until he found her wet and wanting.

"JJ," she gasped as one long finger delved into her, "we can't do this. What about the realtor?"

Chuckling wickedly, he murmured, "Maybe she wasn't due to arrive until later. I'm rotten with details." His arm was like a band of steel around her waist, holding her stationary while a second finger eased into the tight center of her body. Whispering how he wanted to touch her this way and how her passion excited him, he massaged her quivering muscles slowly.

Alex let her forehead rest on his, and wave after wave of explosive sensation crashed over her, sending her beyond the brink of climax. Just as she thought the tender assault had ceased, JJ coaxed her to the edge once more. Mindful of her unsteady condition, he held her securely while the next surge hit, his ragged breath a sweet caress on her cheek.

Struggling to suck oxygen into her lungs, she opened her eyes to find him staring back solemnly, his eyes as dark and turbulent as the deepest ocean.

"I'm going to get you for that," she promised.

"I'll look forward to it." He straightened her clothing considerately and placed a gentle kiss on her mouth, lingering warmly, and she hugged him. "I've missed you since the other night. Have you been deliberately holding back, or is it simply bad timing?"

Alex buried her face in the curve of his neck and sighed. "Both. It was a bit scary making love with you, letting go like that. I wanted it to happen again, but I didn't want to get used to the feeling. You're something else, Mr. Vanzant. I'm sure you've heard that before."

"Honestly, it's never mattered before. That's a little scary for me, too. You shattered me the other night. I've never felt so close—" He stopped, shaking his blond head. "Do you know that you're the only woman I've ever slept with? I mean, curled up to instead of just saying *adios* and leaving?"

She straightened up and inspected his face, checking to see if he was serious.

He grimaced. "Disgusting, huh? I would never take a woman back to my apartment for fear I wouldn't be able to rouse her from it. Not that the rules weren't spelled out by both of us before we got to that point, you understand, but sometimes a female exercises the prerogative to change her mind."

"And you wanted to avoid an awkward situation?" Alex knew she ought to be indignant on behalf of women everywhere, but she realized he had no intention of misleading anyone. If his dates had agreed to a casual night with him, then that was their choice.

"You think I'm loose. There haven't been that many women. Really," JJ stressed. "And our situation is different."

"Mmm-hmm. You invited me into your apartment." A sudden thought occurred. "Or was that just because we couldn't go to my place?"

"No." His face was somber as he told her, "I wanted to

hold you all night. I hated having to drive you home and leave you. I stuck around, didn't I? And I'm counting the days until I can have you beside me every night."

She leaned in and feathered her lips across his. "So am I." Then she grinned. "I would have dearly loved to see you trying to chase a woman out of your apartment, though."

"Don't even joke about it."

A door slammed downstairs, and they scrambled from their cozy embrace to go meet the realtor. The woman chattered politely and expounded on the selling points of the house as Alex trailed her through the kitchen and dining area. The blush staining her cheeks had flamed whilst the agent had shaken hands with her, Alex's paranoid mind certain that the other woman had known just what had been going on upstairs.

JJ had made himself scarce but joined them again just when they returned to the large living room, his dimples flashing devilishly. He dipped his head toward the staircase while the agent wasn't looking and winked broadly.

Alex ignored him.

A few minutes later, she listened to a spectacular description of the blossoming trees in May, and he pretended to inspect the seal on the windows while shooting exaggerated heated glances her way.

Alex pressed her lips together firmly and glared.

"You really are juvenile, you know," she commented once the agent had disappeared to retrieve something from her car. "I may have to reconsider letting you near my children. How will they ever reach maturity if subjected to your influence?"

"I'm harmless." He wrapped strong arms around her and lifted her for a kiss. "Well, will I put the poor woman out of her misery? You like the house?"

"Yes."

A boyish grin lit his features. "My goodness, it's going to be a busy weekend—furniture to pick out and get moved, a kitchen to stock, little boys to get settled away—"

"Wow, she meant it when she said *quick closing.* Ah, about Hank and Billy . . ." Alex disentangled herself and slid to the floor.

"What is it?" JJ's eyes flickered uncertainly. "You haven't told them yet." It was a statement tinged with disappointment.

Wanting to kick herself for being insensitive, she explained, "It was so late last night and then this morning—well, I knew if I told them we were getting married, they wouldn't be calm enough to concentrate in school. So, I asked Mom and Dad not to mention it. I was sort of hoping we could tell them together. Today."

The doubt that had clouded his features dissipated, leaving a crooked grin of understanding in its place. "They do get rather excited, don't they?"

Alex nodded. "I won't get them down off the ceiling for a week, and only then because Santa will be here."

The real estate agent came back, and JJ informed her of the decision to buy. "I want to get moving on the paperwork right away. My family and I would like to be here for Christmas." At Alex's stunned gasp, he enquired, "Is that all right with you, darling?"

"I thought you just meant to get all the big stuff taken care of. *Christmas?* That's next week!"

"Relax," he said disarmingly. "You take care of the wedding arrangements, and I'll see that we have a huge tree in this fantastic room in time for Saint Nick."

The enormity of what he expected to accomplish in a few days hit her full force, a million things cramming onto a mental list in three seconds. Dazed, she forgot the realtor's presence and gave him a chance to change his mind. "Are you absolutely positive about all of this? I mean, it's not too late to back out, JJ."

He studied her for a long moment. "I've never been more certain of anything in my life."

Overwhelmed by all that this man was willing to give her—had already given her—she blinked away the tears blurring her vision and reached up to hug him. Silently, she vowed to find a way to make this Christmas and the ones after better for him than any that had gone before. For this year, she had a pretty good idea what his gift would be—if she could find it with a little help from Nance.

"So, the Mannings aren't as squeaky clean as they would have everyone believe." JJ slapped the folder on his desk and leaned back in his office chair.

After dropping Alex back at her parents' house, he'd gone by the bank and made arrangements for a transfer payment on the house. Then he'd sped by MK Electronics and announced to his shocked friends that not only was he getting hitched, but he fully intended to take advantage of their muscles while moving things into his new home. Jonas had protested jokingly, citing his sore chest and demanding wife. To which JJ had replied, "You can have light duty." Steven had grieved the loss of another good man loudly and made noises about becoming a monk.

Now, JJ smiled in satisfaction at the big black man sitting across from him. "Good work, Spike. I owe you."

"Nah, man. I was happy to do it. Alex doesn't deserve to have those people on her case. This way—" he gestured to the file containing some very potent information about the snobby couple "—she's got leverage."

"This'll be useful if push comes to shove," he agreed, contemplating whether or not to tell his fiancée of this latest development. If the Mannings knew what Spike had dug out of their closet, they'd most likely drop the suit, which meant that Alex's main reason for marrying him would no longer exist. Did he dare risk that she'd insist on using the information and opt for single life once the fear of losing her sons was eliminated? Was it fair of him to take away the choice and trap her in a marriage she may have otherwise never consented to? He had less than two weeks to decide if he could live with the deception and forever wonder if she'd have chosen him anyway.

Aside from that, he'd already pressed his luck with the bloody file he should have destroyed. He'd stood on very thin ice right here in this office and prayed she'd forgive him. If he messed up again, she would never trust him.

"Anything else, boss?"

"Stop calling me *boss*. What are you doing this weekend?"

"Helping you move," replied Spike blandly. "Christa is looking forward to the big party. You know my wife loves to cook for a crowd."

"Did Nance commandeer the entire building?" Frankly, JJ was surprised that so many people were willing to donate their free time to drudge work.

The giant man smiled magnanimously, a slash of perfect pearly whites illuminating his dark face. "Just Jerry and me. Christa volunteered."

"I think you bunch are eager to see me distracted."

"You're already distracted. You need a good woman. We've given our blessing." He chuckled. "You've been a trial to marry off."

"I knew it was a conspiracy." The concern for his unfortunate single status was oddly touching.

"We had discussions." Spike rose and headed for the door. "Later," was all he said before closing it behind him.

It was strange that the people who worked for him

seemed to consider themselves responsible for his personal well-being. He said as much to Alex that afternoon when they picked out furniture for the house. She laughed as if he'd been left out on some private joke and told him that it was his attitude that allowed them to think of him as more than an employer.

"Explain what you mean by that."

She huffed in exasperation. "JJ, you may not have had any family growing up, but you have a tendency to draw people to you."

"Huh?" Confused, he halted in the midst of sofas and chairs to stare at her.

"You don't act like a boss. You take the time to ask interested questions about things other than work. It makes people warm up to you."

"I *am* interested."

"Exactly. How many employers do you know who babysit kids for their employees?"

"But," he argued, "Nance isn't just an employee—and neither is Spike."

Alex chortled hilariously. "You're so blind."

"What? I simply prefer to think of everyone at the firm as coworkers more than underlings. What's wrong with that?"

"Nothing. All I'm saying is, even the secretaries and technicians in the outer offices don't feel intimidated by you, but they still respect you. Probably more because you don't act like you're above them. They *like* you."

JJ chewed on that for a moment. "I don't do anything special, Alex. I only treat people as I'd like to be treated."

"And they reciprocate. So, if you cover for someone who's doing surveillance so that they can spend an evening with their wife on an anniversary, or if you just happen to anonymously take care of another's hydro bill when times are unexpectedly rough—"

"How the hell did Jerry find out about that?" he demanded. Hadn't he been excruciatingly careful with the paperwork?

"That accident took enough of a toll on him without having to pay an arm and a leg while he recovered on sick leave benefits. He got Spike to nose around. Not that he wasn't fairly sure you were the one responsible, he happily informed me."

"Ah, jeez. Does the whole company know?"

"No, just them . . . and Nance . . . and, I guess, me. Don't fret about it. Pretend you don't know." She chuckled delightedly. "I wouldn't have mentioned it but I had to make a point."

"And that would be?"

"Oh, JJ," she lamented, placing soft hands on his cheeks, "you honestly have no concept of your importance to the people around you."

No, he mused, but if it made her look at him with that luminescent glimmer in her eyes, he didn't give a damn if he understood it or not.

They chose a forest-green sofa with matching chairs and a mahogany table set for the living room. Hand-woven rugs to be placed strategically throughout the house were added to the list. JJ insisted on the antique lamps she scrutinized and rejected because of their price, brushing aside her objection by maintaining that he should have some say in what cast light on his reading material.

The decision had been made to move his king-sized bed from the apartment along with his kitchen appliances. Alex selected a set of bunk beds for the boys and then had to be dragged to the department that displayed comforters and sheet sets. She protested that there was no need to buy brand-new things for every room in the house, but ended up doing it anyway. JJ had never expected it would be so difficult to persuade the woman to spend his money, but it was. Every time she chose a pillow or a set of thick towels, she flitted an abashed look his way. He found that he loved giving her things, loved the shyness with which she finally accepted them. And, he acknowledged with some awe, he loved *her.*

The realization hit him as he was examining the brilliant array of engagement rings in the glass case of an exclusive jeweler. It didn't knock him over with the force of an avalanche or frighten the living daylights out of him. Instead, it just crept up on his conscious mind as if it had been lying in wait for him to call it out and confirm its authenticity. A feeling of warm contentment flowed over him, and he closed his eyes briefly to absorb it.

"What are you doing?" Alex, who had disappeared inside a bridal shop, nudged him from his stupor.

"Meditating. Did you find a dress?"

"Mmm-hmm. Simple, ivory, long-sleeved, classic style," she rattled off, hefting a bag containing a large box. "This place is madness. Malls aren't the place to be killing time this close to Christmas."

"Well, as soon as you pick out a ring, we can go home." JJ moved so that she could view the contents of the display case.

Her mouth parted soundlessly, and she immediately shook her head. "I don't need a ring—"

Taking the bag from her unresisting fingers, he pushed her to the counter. "I want you to have one."

"Then you choose. Please," she said, forestalling an argument.

"All right," he conceded, "but it's not going back." He scanned the sparkling arrangement again, his gaze stopping on a ring that he knew was meant to be placed on her left hand. The diamonds were small and tasteful—not baubly as some he'd seen—and they clustered around a slightly bigger sapphire fashioned in the shape of a heart. The band in which the stones were set was gold and had a subtle, swirling design carved into its smoothness. "That one." He directed the hovering jeweler to remove it from the case.

It was just the right fit for Alex's finger, sliding easily over her knuckle as JJ gently put it on. He waited for her reaction and was stunned to see her lovely eyes shimmering with tears for the second time that day. "Alex?"

"It's beautiful," she whispered, tilting her hand so that the blue gem glinted brilliantly. "It reminds me of your eyes."

"We'll take it," he said when he managed to pull his gaze from hers.

That evening, they sat with Hank and Billy and prepared them for the upcoming nuptials. As expected, they were thrilled and pounced on JJ gleefully. Alex smiled and tossed a glance skyward before going to answer the phone. When she returned, however, the smile had vanished.

"Elizabeth," she muttered hours later. The woman was a bona fide witch. After a three-minute diatribe about how unsuitable Alex was to be the mother of her *precious* Darryl's children, she remembered to politely ask how they were. Then, not waiting for a response, went on to bemoan the fact that her only other offspring had decided not to give her any grandchildren. Patrice, Darryl's sister, had become too caught up in her modeling career to give even a passing thought to the whims of her parents, thus leaving them no other choice but to rely on Hank and Billy to *uphold the sterling reputation that goes along with the Manning name.* Obviously, this could not be accomplished as long as they lived with their very unfit mother.

Alex was fit to be tied. She'd coldly informed the woman

that she was getting married soon to a wonderful man who was going to make an even more wonderful father. The sense of satisfaction she'd experienced when there was a bewildered silence on the other end had been short-lived. Elizabeth had revved her engines and let go with every bit of spite and venom she could muster. She'd screeched in Alex's ear that it was all a farce, that no judge in his right mind wouldn't see through her charade of a marriage. Totally fed up with the selfish hag, Alex had slammed the phone down and returned to the living room.

JJ had taken one look at her wan complexion and known something was amiss but had waited for the boys to wind down and get settled in bed before broaching the subject. His expression hardened into a cold mask when she told him about the phone call.

"Forget it, Alex. I'm not going to let them separate you from your sons, and truth be known, no court is going to let it happen either. They're way out in left field with this suit, but they figure you won't even go to court if they intimidate you enough." He held her snugly and stroked the rigid line of her back.

"Are you sure you want to take on all of my troubles, JJ?" Confounded by his unwavering support, she was compelled to keep giving him an excuse to bail out of the arrangement.

"Sweetheart, once we're husband and wife, those problems will cease to exist." He sat on one end of the couch and pulled her across his lap, fluffing a pillow and placing it behind her head.

From her prone position, she stared up at him and just enjoyed the feel of his strong hand as it soothed the frown lines away. Her eyes drifted closed, and she surrendered to the fatigue that was invading her body. An instant later, her attention was riveted when he began to speak.

CHAPTER TEN

JJ wasn't sure why he felt the need to unburden himself to her at that particular time. Maybe it was to make her understand how much he truly longed for the acceptance and warmth of a family. Or perhaps he just meant to reassure her that he needed her as badly as she seemed to need him. Whatever it was, it eased the self-protective shield aside and let him recount the details of his childhood with unrelenting candor.

He entrusted her with the tale of the frightened, mutinous eight-year-old boy who'd had to clean his mother up after her binges and steal food from the grocer's because she'd drunk the welfare money. The strange feeling of guilt he'd carried all those years because he'd been so relieved that she'd taken him to the orphanage seemed to disintegrate with every word he articulated.

Alex lay quietly in his arms and listened as he described the kindness of the nuns and their unfailing optimism that the next foster home would be the one he'd settle into for sure.

Recollection had him smiling telling her about Addy and her rosy cheeks. But then he scowled a little while he explained that hours spent in Mrs. Botnik's itty-bitty closet was the reason he couldn't stand enclosed spaces for any length of time. He sketched a chilling picture of a foster father who liked young boys in a none-too-paternal fashion, relating how he'd chomped down on the pervert's arm when he'd tried to touch him, thereby securing a guaranteed one-way ticket back to the boys' home.

JJ recalled the worst and the best vividly—the transitory foster homes in between were one gigantic blur. He eventually halted his ramblings self-consciously, and the woman in his lap dashed away the wetness from her brown eyes.

"I didn't tell you any of this to upset you, Alex," he said, slightly alarmed. "I only wanted you to see what a gift you're giving me by agreeing to be my wife. This can be a new beginning for the both of us."

"Yes." She lifted her arms for a hug. "A new beginning, Jesse," she whispered in his ear. "I just hope you're not disappointed."

Drawing a deep breath, he buried his nose in her silky hair and promised, "You won't have to worry about that." The possibility that she would find *him* wanting in some aspect was more likely, he surmised. This relationship thing was very much a seat-of-the-pants operation for him. He assumed that Alex knew what she was doing and resolved to take his cues from her.

"I'm sorry." She sniffed delicately. "I seem to have been plagued with crying spurts all day."

"I noticed that. Are you sure you're not pregnant?"

"Yes, I'm sure. It's just that so much has happened so fast—I haven't been able to take it all in. I feel . . . *muddled.*"

JJ ignored the desire rising in him, adjusting her so she wouldn't detect the growing bulge in his lap. "Well," he mumbled past the thickness in his throat, "we'll take care of the blood tests and the marriage license tomorrow. The house is apparently taking care of itself with everyone descending on it this weekend to help and—ah, don't wiggle like that, Alex."

"Hmm? Like this?"

"I have to drive home." His voice was hoarse, and he had difficulty respiring.

"You could stay here—in my room."

"Not with your parents down the hall." He gasped. "Get your tongue out of my ear."

"We're practically married."

"I don't care. I'd feel like a heel in the morning." The hot kisses being trailed up his neck were almost his undoing.

"I'd still respect you." Alex gave a soft laugh and covered his mouth hungrily with hers.

"I have to go." Groaning when she squirmed to entice him, he insisted, "I'm leaving now." Pause. "I am."

Eventually, he stumbled out to the jeep with most of his clothes in place.

Saturday came, and the new house was flooded with people. JJ's *employees* had arrived promptly at nine with their respective families and significant others. Steven showed up dressed completely in black and stared balefully at the prospective groom, claiming he was deeply aggrieved at being left the last bachelor of the male trio. Jonas and Viv trekked in after him with Eleuthera and her beau, Dr. Reynolds. Jonas' uncle, Michael Hunt, even put in an appearance with his new bride, Dottie.

By noon, the living room furniture had been delivered from the department store and now sat on beautifully woven rugs, JJ's bed had made the trip across town and was laboriously lugged upstairs by the men, and the appliances had been arranged in the kitchen once every surface had been scoured clean.

Pizzas were picked up by Lorna and George, who were awestruck at the sight of their daughter's new home. Then the whole group crowded around the newly purchased dining room table and lined up at the kitchen counters to partake of the cheesy concoctions.

The rest of the day was spent cleaning the rest of the house and the garage and seeing to it that the phone land lines were in working order.

Christa, Spike's beloved and mother of two darling girls, offered to come back the following day and help cart in the bed linens and such. On the verge of refusing politely, for they'd all been so generous with their time, Alex was overruled before one word got out by Nance.

"There's still tons to do," the skip-tracer stated. "I think we can whip up a spread tomorrow in that huge kitchen. How about it, Christa?"

The stunning black woman added in her Jamaican accent, "That's just what I was thinking. I'd love to get my hands on that lovely set of cookware — break it in, so to speak." Christa owned and operated a successful restaurant on the waterfront and was an outstanding chef.

The whole room perked up anew at the mention of her offer and vowed to be back the next day to finish getting things settled.

Alex giggled, a bit lightheaded after the day's activity, and glanced over at her fiancé. He was grinning and joking with Nance's husband and two teenage sons, his rumpled sweater and jeans not detracting from his appeal at all. In fact, she thought he looked distinctly huggable.

Viv bumped her gently. "Methinks you'll have a bunch of us again tomorrow."

Smiling, she replied, "I'm hoping for it. We need the help, and JJ is in his element."

"So are you." Her friend eyed her closely. "You seem happy, Alex."

Lifting a shoulder, she truthfully answered, "I am. I didn't expect to be in this strange situation, but it's going to work out, I think."

Viv squeezed her warmly. "JJ keeps watching you. I believe he's smitten."

"No, he isn't." *But I wouldn't complain if he was.* She was still slightly amazed at the ease with which he interacted with other people. Their conversation in the mall came back to her, and she smiled when recalling how genuinely stumped he'd been as she'd tried to explain that he was valued by others simply because he was who he was. Alex was convinced that apart from being best friend, surrogate brother, employer, and future husband, JJ Vanzant was a family man without a family. And that was definitely going to change if she had any say in the matter.

"He's smitten, I tell you." Viv reminded her that she was still there. "You're not much better off!"

"I don't know what you mean."

"Hmph!"

The friendly group broke up shortly and promised to be back after lunch the next day. Hank and Billy were worn out and didn't argue when Alex shooed them home with her parents. Left alone with JJ, she plunked down next to him on the new sofa and sighed.

"Want to go try my bed?" he slyly enquired.

"I've tried it."

"Not in that position."

Several positions came to mind, only half of them involving the bed. "We still need to finish stocking the refrigerator. One more run to the grocer's."

"How domestic," was his dry response.

"Get used to it."

JJ gazed around him and idly wondered what he'd done to deserve a life that was shaping up so nicely. His friends were gathered around him after an enormous Caribbean-style Sunday dinner prepared in his comfortable new home, the conversation jousting back and forth between hockey and shop talk. Alex passed by his chair now and then to casually touch him, her easy manner adding to the cloak of intimacy surrounding them even as the house thrummed with the presence of others.

Hank and Billy had crawled into his lap and dozed off, one dark head on each of his shoulders. The scene should have been chaos, what with kids around and grown-ups laughing good-naturedly. Instead, an unfamiliar calm stole over him, and he found himself just enjoying the sound of other people talking.

That was the precise moment his nagging inner voice chose to kick him in the teeth. *Don't get too comfortable, buddy! You still haven't told Alex about the Manning file.*

Shut up. There's still time. I'll tell her after Christmas.

Sure, sure. As long as she doesn't hear it from Spike first — but you took care of that, didn't you?

Damn straight!

Although, Spike had looked at him a little oddly before agreeing not to bring it up in front of Alex.

So, I'd like to spend the holidays with her and not worry if she'll up and leave when I let it be known that I have foolproof ammunition against her in-laws. Go ahead, call me a selfish bastard!

Selfish bastard! the pesky voice obliged.

Fine. Now, bugger off!

Later, as he carried a sleeping Hank from the jeep, he pondered again the wisdom of keeping Alex in the dark. Surely, a few days couldn't hurt. It wasn't as if he planned on going through with the wedding without telling her, period. He'd give her a chance to back out before the *I do's*, just not until he'd shown her what their life together could be like.

Billy was changed and tucked in by the time JJ had deposited his brother on the bed. He was a tad slower than Alex in these things, but he figured he'd learn fast. Besides, the woman had loads more experience.

Hank stirred and opened bleary eyes when his head hit the pillow. "JJ?" he mumbled.

"Yeah, sport, time for bed." He ruffled the black hair affectionately and turned to leave.

"I have a question," Hank of the never-ending curiosity stated, halting him in his tracks. "Is it okay for us to call you Dad? After you and Mom get married, I mean."

JJ's heart stopped. He threw Alex a helpless glance, silently pleading for some assistance. She shrugged almost imperceptibly and smiled.

"It's okay with me." As she passed him in the doorway, she murmured, "It suits you."

The sincerity in that small endorsement was all the encouragement he needed. Willing his vocal cords to untie themselves, he ambled back to Hank's bedside and quietly told him, "You can call me whatever you want."

"I'll call you Dad. I'm glad you're going to live with us." Hank sat up and reached for him. "I love you."

JJ caught him as thin arms clamped hard around his waist, holding fast to the boy he'd come to adore. For a long time, he sat on the edge of the bed and hugged him before the words he'd never uttered to another living soul escaped the tight knot in his throat.

"I love you, too."

Alex was tidying up the kitchen when he emerged. A pot of coffee was percolating on the counter, four mugs lined up next to it.

"One for the road? Mom and Dad are having a cup before bed. Decaf," she added wryly. "Everything okay?"

"Sure," he croaked.

Alex considered him thoughtfully. "Hank didn't make you uncomfortable, did he? If you'd rather the boys kept using your first name, I'd understand."

"No, he just surprised me. I never imagined that something so simple could feel so . . . monumental." He shook his head wonderingly. "Come to that, I never envisioned anyone wanting to have me for a father. That blows me away."

Slipping her arms around him, she remarked, "It shouldn't. You're a good man, JJ. A bit goofy, but I think that only adds to your charm."

"See? I knew you liked me all along!"

They sat sipping coffee and discussed the wedding with Lorna and George. The ceremony would take place at the Mackenzie estate, much in the same fashion as Jonas and Viv's. Eleuthera had made the offer to use the solarium generously, claiming she loved another excuse to ring in the New Year with a bash—that being the ball-reception to follow. Alex and JJ let her railroad them into it, knowing they'd have trouble booking a chapel on such short notice anyway. They'd objected to putting anyone to trouble, but Eleuthera had waved away the protest with a bejeweled hand. If there was one thing Jonas' mother loved to do, it was orchestrate a shindig.

The guest list for the wedding was not long. Alex's parents were giving her away. JJ had invited Nance and her family, Jerry and his girlfriend, Spike's clan, and Michael and Dottie Hunt.

Cass and Caro, who had spent the weekend in Bay de Chance, were thrilled with the prospect of standing up for Alex—if a little baffled by the early date. They swore to be at her side with bells on when she'd rung them an hour ago, hoping the short notice wouldn't inconvenience them. But, like all of the Kincaid family, they seemed prepared for anything to happen at any given time.

Viv had tearfully accepted her place as matron of honor days ago, and JJ had frankly been embarrassed when she'd cried all over him and the bride-to-be, patting her hand awkwardly. Jonas had mouthed, "I think we may be pregnant already," which, to a man's way of thinking, explained everything.

Steven and the redhead had been allotted the groomsmen positions because he couldn't decide which to ask to act as best man. Therefore, JJ was left racking his brain for someone to complete the wedding party and decided that he'd somehow manage to have Hank and Billy stand next to him — two best men were a little unconventional, but who really cared? Alex didn't and said they'd be like a couple of helium balloons when he asked them.

The talk turned to Alex's plans to keep working after the New Year. Lorna and George thought she should stay home, but JJ cast his vote with the future Mrs. Vanzant.

"Whatever you want is fine with me," he stated firmly. "Besides, I'd like some notice before I have to find another secretary."

"Hah! That's your main concern, not to be left stranded and confused by the alphabet!" she charged, smiling.

"Not so. I still think you ought to consider finishing your degree. You did say you only had one semester left. You don't have to decide right away." He rose and took the empty mugs to the sink. Behind him, George and Lorna made noises about going to bed.

"It's very sweet of you to think of me, but it's such an expense," Alex said when they'd gone. "And I couldn't very well ask Mom and Dad to look after the boys while I'm in class. They've done so much for me as it is. I feel like I've been a drain on what should be the most relaxed time of their lives."

"You seem to be forgetting something," JJ commented dryly. He dropped back into his seat and placed an arm along the back of hers. "In a week or so, you won't have to worry about paying all of your own bills, taking care of the boys alone and whatnot. I'll be helping with the responsibilities. Besides, if you want to go back to school, Hank and Billy are in their own during the day, and when summer comes, we'll have to find a regular sitter while we're working. Evening classes wouldn't be a problem since I'm usually home, anyway." He leaned over and tweaked her nose. "Stop seeing obstacles where there aren't any."

"None but the Mannings. Getting married may put them off a bit, but if they have a mind to secure custody, the next best thing to an unemployed, unfit mother is an absent one. They'll say I'm never at home."

"Judges don't look at these situations in black and white, Alex. Don't worry about Elizabeth and what's-his-face. We'll run them off." If they weren't sensible enough to back off on their own, he'd damned well give them an excuse.

The following morning provided the perfect opportunity to spell it out for them. He only wished the boys had already left for school before the older couple arrived.

The scene on the front steps of the Eldrich home told its own story. Hank and Billy were clinging to their mother, red-faced and sobbing, as Elizabeth and her shadow husband stared them down.

"It's all a ruse, Alex," the woman was yelling. "This mystery man you've come up with isn't interested in marrying you or becoming a father to my grandchildren. How utterly cruel of you to let them believe otherwise."

"Excuse me," JJ interjected calmly. "Alex, if you'll put the kids in the jeep, we can drop them instead of waiting for a bus." He quirked an eyebrow pleasantly as she took the hint and led them out of earshot.

"Who the devil are you?" demanded Elizabeth.

"As far as you're concerned," he replied conversationally, "I am the Devil. Now leave before I have you arrested for trespassing and harassment."

"That's ridiculous! We've every right to be here, Mr. —"

"Vanzant. That's V-A-N-Z-A-N-T. I'm Alex's fiancé and I plan to make sure that neither of you cause her grief. If you doubt my sincerity," he smiled, all teeth, "just know that I have some very revealing photos of you, Gerard, and some extremely incriminating financial documents with your wife's signature on them. Maybe you'd like to persuade her to avoid spending any time in jail?" With that, he left them staring blank-faced at each other and got into the jeep.

"Is it true, Mom? Is she gonna take us from you?" Billy was huddled beside his brother, his bottom lip trembling uncontrollably.

"No, sweetie, she was just being nasty." Alex threw a panic-stricken look his way, and he pulled out of the driveway, spewing dirty snow all over the Mannings' gray sedan.

"But she said JJ didn't love us and youse was gonna get a di-di—"

"Divorce," supplied Hank sullenly.

"Yeah." Billy hiccupped loudly and scrubbed his sleeve beneath his nose.

Seeing the distress their mother was in, JJ tried to reassure them. "Billy, your mom and I are getting married for good. There won't be any divorce, and nobody is going to take you from us. Okay?"

"Good, 'cause I don't like them!"

"Me, neither!" echoed Hank.

"Then it's unanimous," muttered JJ, "I can't stomach 'em either." He glanced over at Alex, who had closed her eyes and was drawing breaths to steady herself. "All right?"

Mutely, she nodded, the color beginning to return to her pale face. "*Snobs!*" she hissed lowly.

"Glad to see your mood is improving, sweetheart. I thought the fight might have gone out of you," he mused with a crooked grin.

"Not in this lifetime."

And definitely not in his, JJ swore some time later as he lifted a fist and pounded on a hotel room door. He placed a finger over the peephole when he heard a shuffling sound inside. The door cracked open a fraction, and Gerard's long nose appeared between two bulging eyeballs. Before he could slam it again, JJ shoved his foot in the gap.

"Take off the chain, Mr. Manning. We have things to discuss, and I'm sure you'd prefer to do it in private."

"All right, but just for a minute. Elizabeth will be back from lunch soon." The stooped man shut the door and unhooked the chain, moving farther into the room when JJ entered and locked them both in.

"Why don't we put an end to this nonsense now, Gerard," he said mildly. "I don't think you'd like your high fallutin' wife to know about those evenings you've been, shall we say, getting in touch with your feminine side?"

Gerard gulped visibly, his prominent Adam's apple bobbing up and down at the mention of his cross-dressing fetish. "How did you know about that?"

"Let's just call it providence that certain pictures of you in the before, during, and after stages of preparation fell into my hands. Some fellow *femme* must have wanted to record the beauty process for posterity, I guess. Harold, I believe, was his name." The owner of the nightclub that featured drag queens every Wednesday had been happy to oblige Spike with the colorful photos. For a small fee, of course.

"Elizabeth doesn't know. When you referred to it this morning, she thought you meant—"

"That I had some security video, perhaps? Of a certain accountant and his spouse coming and going at the firm where he works—after hours, when there's no one around?" JJ experienced a perverse sense of pleasure as he witnessed the blood draining from the other man's face.

"You couldn't possibly have her on tape, she wasn't there. It was only me." Sweat broke out on Gerard's forehead, and his gaze darted frantically around the room, as if he was searching for an avenue of escape.

"No, but Elizabeth signed the deposit slips at the bank. I don't think your employers are going to have to tax their math skills to put it together. Just how long have you been siphoning off the accounts, anyway? A year? Two?" JJ bent down to fix a stony stare on the man who'd slumped defeatedly on the edge of the bed. "And how long before they discover what I know? Maybe they know already."

Gerard whipped off his glasses jerkily and swept an arm over his eyes. "Damn her!" he muttered in a shaky voice. "If she wasn't so obsessed with having everything, we wouldn't be in this mess. Spend, spend, spend. I never wondered where Darryl picked up the habit."

Taken aback at the last statement, JJ straightened and folded his arms as the shrunken man tattled on.

"*Oh, but we have to go here, Gerard, the Baxters are going,*" he mimicked in a high-pitched tone. "*We simply must buy that car, Gerard. Your boss will be so impressed!* and *Oh, but I need a new wardrobe. Whatever will everyone think if I wear last year's clothes?*"

A flicker of pity rose up in JJ, but he squelched it immediately. If the man had trouble standing up to his overbearing wife to the point that he'd been coerced into criminal acts, he was going to have to learn to exhibit some backbone. Grand theft and larceny were serious business with serious penalties attached.

"Well, Elizabeth doesn't need to hear about your secret cavortings. But I strongly suggest you convince her to drop the custody suit. I've a feeling it won't be too much longer before you have some *real* legal battles to worry over." Especially since he'd spoken to the accounting firm personally, JJ smugly recalled. "It's a crying shame you let her talk you into stealing that money, Gerard. It was her idea, wasn't it?"

"Does it matter?" came the broken reply. "I went along with it. I'm as guilty as she."

"Yes, you are." He turned to leave, confident that the Mannings would cease to be a bother after today. "Oh, by the way," he threw over one shoulder, unable to resist a parting shot, "You do make a rather stunning woman."

CHAPTER ELEVEN

"The boys are so used to sleeping in the same room," Alex humourously remarked the day before Christmas Eve, "that they nearly pitched a fit when I said they could each have their own if they wanted. I'm sure they'll grow out of that in a few years."

They had moved the last of their clothes and personal items into the house and now lay, arms and legs entwined, on the new couch. A fire burned in the grate, the flames dancing across the darkened room intimately.

Hank and Billy were tucked in upstairs for their first night in the house, sleeping soundly after JJ had indulged them with two bedtime stories.

"Tired?" he asked, stroking her hair.

Alex cuddled into his chest and inhaled the scent of him. "A little." The day had finally eased into darkness, the hours ticking by more slowly as she relished the feel of his arms.

"Tomorrow, I'm taking the boys to get a tree. Want to come?" JJ mumbled against her forehead.

"Mmm. Should be fun." Then, she remembered the important errand she had to run. "But I was hoping I could borrow your jeep for an hour, say two o'clock?"

"You have a license?"

She punched him playfully. "Naturally. I just haven't had occasion to use it lately."

"I knew that. I could drive you where you want to go."

"Not this time."

"Ah, my mysterious present. What have you and Nance

been up to?" He abruptly pinned her beneath him, grinning at her surprised *oh*. "Tell me."

"Nope."

"I'll guess."

"You've been trying for days." There was no way he'd figure it out, not in a million years.

"Will I like it?" JJ shifted, aligning his body more closely with hers.

"I think you will."

"Something I made reference to?"

"Yes," Alex solemnly told him, hoping she hadn't been wrong to go looking for it. "Something I believe you've wanted for a long time."

"You aren't going to tell me?"

"No." She smiled up at him and gasped softly when he lifted her thigh, guiding it around his hip. The evidence of his arousal swelled against the center of her desire, turning her insides to molten lava. "I can't be coaxed."

JJ laughed. "We'll see." He kissed her and bore down on her lustily, rubbing his erection erotically over her. She moaned and wrapped both legs around lean hips, returning the friction with heated fervor. He tore his mouth free and swore.

"What's the matter, lover?" Alex was the one to laugh this time. "Can't handle having the tables turned?" She thrilled at the way his eyes stormed passionately and his hard cheeks flushed with a tinge of red.

Rolling off her, he stood and scooped her from the couch, cutting short her startled shriek with his hungry mouth. "I think we ought to finish this little skirmish upstairs, minx. We'll see who can't handle it."

In the end, it was a draw.

When morning light filtered in through the slit in the bedroom curtains, Alex propped herself on one elbow and gazed down at the sleeping man beside her. His blond hair was tousled, as were the sheets around his waist, and a bristly beard was beginning on his square chin and jaw, his mouth parted slightly on a subdued snore. She inched closer and slid a thigh between his rougher ones, a hand automatically seeking the pulse of his strong heart. She caressed his broad chest gently, taking advantage of his unconscious state as she looked her fill of this magnificent man. Not for the first time, she wondered what he saw in her when he could have any woman he fancied on a platter.

JJ's piercing blue eyes caught her examination, and he smiled drowsily. "Morning," he whispered, pulling her over him.

"Good morning."

"What were you staring at?" His body was waking up faster than his brain, and he was making absolutely certain that she was aware of it.

"You." Alex took his steely length inside her and braced her hands on the mattress. "You're beautiful." She shook her head when he seemed ready to disagree and began loving him slowly, taking him deeper with every stroke. His eyes remained locked on hers even when he came, burning hotly, his seed filling her.

Alex kissed his face and neck, then his shoulders and chest, and he drifted back into a deep slumber. A glistening bead of moisture squeezed from between his lashes, and she captured the salty drop on the tip of one finger before bringing it to her mouth to taste in wonderment. "Beautiful."

"Mom said to let him sleep." The loud whisper was not ten inches from his ear.

JJ fought back a grin as Billy ignored his brother's admonishment and scrambled onto the foot of the bed. He plunked his little body on JJ's ankles and bounced twice.

"He gotta get up soon. All the trees will be gone." Billy crawled up his prone body and stopped on his stomach. "JJ? Uh, I mean, *Daddy*? You awake?" A small hand patted his cheek.

"Get off him, Billy. You'll squish him."

Laughter rumbled in JJ's chest at the thought of either of the miniature mites crushing him. He reached out an arm and grabbed Hank, tugging him onto the thick comforter. Mindful of his state of undress beneath the blankets, JJ wrapped them tightly around his waist, then tickled the yelping boys and growled gleefully.

"Breakfast is ready," Alex interrupted from the doorway. "Hank, didn't I say not to wake him? Never mind. Go downstairs and eat your eggs." She plucked the still breathless and chortling whirlwinds off the bed and smacked a kiss on each cheek. When she released them, they raced for the door and blew down the hall.

JJ laced his fingers behind his head and watched her through heavy-lidded eyes. He recalled how she'd looked earlier as she made love to him, her black hair falling over her shoulders, breasts heaving temptingly. Something in her dark eyes had held him fascinated, an indefinable emotion that was as spellbinding as the woman herself. He'd begun to hope she might be coming to love him just a little, that maybe she was letting go of her late husband's memory — or, at the very least, was making room for new ones with him.

"Well?" she prodded now, her eyes twinkling, "Are you getting up, or do we have to drag you out of bed?"

"I thought you could try handling me like you did a couple hours ago."

"That wouldn't get you out of bed."

"No," he agreed, grinning hugely.

Alex strode to the side of the bed and whipped back the

covers. Then, seeing his obvious state of arousal, threw them down again. "You're insatiable."

"Mmm-hmm. It's the curse you've bestowed upon me." He sighed.

"I can remove it."

"No, no. I like it."

"How unfortunate that it prevents you from getting up."

"I'm up!" JJ reminded her.

"I saw." Shaking her head, she made for the door. "I'm going down to make our breakfast. Don't force me to come searching for you again."

"Yes, darling."

The shower was cold and stinging. He stuck his head under the spray and pondered that for discretion's sake, he'd have to start wearing pajama bottoms. He was unused to waking up with two children by his bed.

JJ soaped up a lather and chuckled to himself. He'd once thought that kids would be an annoyance on a regular basis, entities to avoid in the early hours of daylight. The feelings that had flooded him when Hank and Billy had launched their warmth onto his bed, however, hadn't been irritating at all. In fact, he'd experienced a rush of pure delight when they'd howled and hugged him out of his semi-conscious condition. He was becoming accustomed to this paternal stuff.

The four of them hunted down a Christmas tree in under three hours, which JJ considered was no small feat given the indecisiveness of the tiny tikes. Hank wanted an enormous pine, then a runty three-footer. Billy insisted on an anemic-looking fir but said he'd settle for the tree of his mother's choice since she'd picked a good one last year.

Ultimately, the tree they concurred would be best in the living room was a six-foot pine from the back of the lot. Its branches were thick and full and healthy. JJ and the salesman tied it to the top of the jeep and marked it with a red tape.

On the ride home, the boys pleaded with their mother to stop for burgers at their favorite joint, and she conceded, rolling her eyes expressively as they cheered.

The tree fit into its stand without much fuss, and JJ pushed it to one side of the fireplace. They stood back and scrutinized it for a few minutes before declaring it perfect.

Billy wanted to decorate it immediately, but Alex over-ruled him, urging them to eat their takeout food first and wait until she came back from running her *errand*. JJ pestered her about the gift to no avail and finally gave up, wandering off to find the lights and decorations they'd bought the day before.

"I can put these on while you're gone, right? Just the lights?"

Alex instructed gravely, "Not with your gloves on this time."

"Good idea." He halted in front of the tree and peered over his shoulder to find her watching him, an odd air about her. "What?" he pressed when her mouth opened soundlessly.

"Uh, it's about your present." Uncertainty clouded her eyes as she continued, "I just wanted you to know that I have your best interests at heart. I mean, it seemed like a good plan at the time, but I may have overstepped."

JJ frowned, wondering what could be so complicated about a simple gift. "We're getting married next week, Alex. I don't think there's any area in our relationship left to tres-pass on, do you?" *Unless you count your first husband.*

"I guess not. I only wanted to give you something special. I hope you don't think I'm meddling or anything." She con-centrated on yanking her gloves on, apparently edgier than he realized.

He ambled over and nuzzled her cheek until she glanced up. "You sure I can't drive you?"

"I'm sure." Those big brown eyes tugged at his heartstrings. "I won't be long," she promised and kissed him tenderly.

Just as she exited the drive, a midnight blue minivan appeared from the opposite direction, and he smiled, thinking the delivery of the Christmas present he'd bought for her had barely survived detection. Another car bearing the logo of a dealership followed the van up to the house. JJ directed them to the garage and turned to encounter two sets of curious eyes.

"Who's that?" Hank enquired innocently.

"Uh, that's some men bringing your mom's gift. It's a surprise, so you have to keep it a secret." They nodded vigorously, so he put their outdoor clothes on, and the three of them went to *ooh* and *aah* over the van. JJ closed the garage door to hide it from Alex and thanked the salesmen for bringing it out. "Remember," he admonished the boys in a gentle way, "not a word to your mother."

Again, they bobbed their heads excitedly.

Thirty minutes later, the phone rang. Gerard Manning curtly informed him that he and his wife were dropping the suit.

"That's wise of you," JJ remarked with approval. "I'm sure you know that Hank and Billy will be properly taken care of."

"Yes, yes. Elizabeth and I are sorry for causing any grief." Then he rang off abruptly, not even enquiring after his grandchildren.

"Merry Christmas to you, too." JJ went back to the living room and found the boys chattering animatedly about the lights, the abbreviated phone call still on his mind.

Alex could now have a completely worry-free holiday. He

imagined the look on her face when he told her she didn't have to be troubled with the looming prospect of a custody battle—she'd be able to enjoy the next few days without dealing with the disquieting notion of losing her sons, without the financial strain of the last year, without feeling forced to marry a man she didn't . . . love.

He stalled in the middle of stringing the last miniature bulbs on the tree. A cold knot had formed in the pit of his stomach, much like the one that made itself known when he got claustrophobic. Oxygen was indeed at a minimum, as well. The room spun out of focus momentarily, and that dreaded rush of water thundered in his ears.

"Daddy!" Billy's voice seemed to come from a great distance, although when he opened his eyes it was to find the little boy leaning trustingly against his leg. "Is you gonna help us make a snowman after?"

Sucking in a lungful of much-needed air, he tried a smile. "You bet."

Billy went back to sorting ornaments with his brother, thankfully oblivious to the turmoil raging inside the grown-up.

JJ shoved the unpleasant thoughts to the back of his mind. Just because Alex no longer needed him as a shield against the Mannings, didn't mean she didn't need him at all. He was obligated to tell her they'd dropped the suit. For now, he'd have to pray that it wouldn't affect her decision to marry him.

The ugly feeling of unrest persisted, however, until the jeep rumbled in the drive, and he threw back the door to welcome her in from the cold. She wasn't alone.

An elderly couple of about sixty climbed down from the vehicle. The man was tall and slender with a shock of curly white hair blowing in the frigid breeze. The woman was short and pleasingly plump, her face hidden by a woolen scarf and cap. The spring in her step prodded JJ's memory, but he failed to recognize where he'd seen her before.

It was slightly disturbing to see Alex and the old man retrieve suitcases from the back of the jeep. Had she invited guests to stay with them for their first Christmas as a family? Strangers to intrude on the time that should have been especially for them? No, she wouldn't. She hadn't, he confirmed, when the little lady preceded Alex up the walk and into the house. JJ stepped aside for the trio to enter and closed the door on the winter wind, his gaze glued to the bundled-up matron.

"Addy?" he whispered in disbelief. "Is that really you?"

Those sparkling hazel eyes beamed up at him merrily. She slipped off her knitted cap and scarf, revealing the rosy cheeks he remembered so well. "How are you, darling?"

Stunned, it took him a second to formulate an intelligent response. Dimly aware that Alex had ushered the boys and the older gentleman to the kitchen, he blurted, "Fine. You've met—" He cast a searching glance over his shoulder and confirmed the living room was indeed deserted.

"Alex? Yes, dear. Such a sweet girl." Addy's gaze turned watery. "Oh my, I've missed you." She pressed a weathered hand over her mouth, and JJ bent down to envelop her in a bear hug.

"I've missed you, too," he managed to murmur past the lump in his throat. He squeezed his burning eyes shut and held on to his foster mother, not caring if he bawled like a baby. "Where have you been?" he asked, easing back a trifle.

Addy dabbed at his wet cheeks with her hanky and then at her own. "It's a long story, but we have lots of time."

"I hope those bags over there mean you're staying a while?"

"If you don't mind, dear. Albert and I don't have any children of our own, so when Alex asked if we'd like to spend the holidays here . . . well, we couldn't resist."

"Oh, yes," JJ said, relieving her of her coat. "That's your husband?"

Nodding her gray head, she clarified, "I met Albert Wentworth shortly after I moved to PEI—I go by that name now—and we married right away. He's retired from the military these days, and we travel quite a bit. It was nothing to hop on a plane when Alex called." She reached up and touched his face affectionately. "I never forgot you, you know. I wanted to take you with me when I left, but the province wouldn't allow it. A thirty-something widow wasn't considered a good candidate for adopting children back then."

JJ paused at that bit of information. "I didn't know you wanted to adopt me."

"I most certainly did. You were a darling little boy, if a bit rough around the edges. But not only did they deem me unsuitable parent material on a permanent basis, the necessary paperwork hadn't been on file for you to be adopted."

Yes, his mother had seen to that—or *not* seen to it in this case.

"Anyway," Addy continued, "I tried to find out how you were doing several times but I wasn't allowed to have any information. After a time, I figured you probably had forgotten me and didn't need to be reminded."

"I thought the same about you."

"We won't stay if it bothers you," she offered, her discerning gaze laced with understanding.

JJ enfolded her in another great hug. "No, stay. I'm glad you're here," he assured her, bussing her still smooth cheek exuberantly. "Now, introduce me to your beau."

Albert was rather easy-going for a military man. He was telling jokes to Hank and Billy when they entered the kitchen, faded blue eyes glittering with mirth. He stood and shook hands with JJ solemnly, his grasp firm and warm.

"Addy always talked about you right from the first day we met," he embarrassed JJ by saying. "I feel as if I know you already."

"Well, I hope you're comfortable enough to stick around for the wedding next week, sir."

"Call me Albert." He smiled. "I think my wife and I would love that."

They sat around the table trading bits and pieces of personal data for an hour. JJ caught Alex eyeing him hesitantly and grinned, communicating his genuine delight over her gift to him. He couldn't believe she'd tracked Addy for him. The love he felt for the dark-haired beauty swelled in his chest, growing deeper and more overwhelming than anything he'd known before. She blushed and dipped her head at the intense scrutiny, seeming abashed that he openly displayed such a tender attitude.

Trimming the tree was a boisterous event, the boys cheerfully hanging the ornaments and stringing garland. Addy and Albert joined in the festive activity with great enthusiasm. When it came time to place the bright star on top, Billy and Hank argued over which of them got to do the honors.

"I think," JJ interjected diplomatically, "that your mother should put the star up." They gave in to his suggestion with a minimum of whining and impatiently urged Alex to crown the tree.

"I can't reach up there," she protested. A startled laugh erupted from her when JJ hoisted her high on his chest. "All right, a little closer." The star fit snugly on the top and glowed white when the lights were plugged in.

"Wow!" breathed Billy. "That's the best tree we ever had!"

"Uh-huh," the usually articulate Hank chimed in.

Alex dimmed the lights for the full effect. A multitude of

colors glimmered on the branches and reflected around the room—the garland and angel's hair enriched the rainbow even more. They were all adamant that it was the most majestic, beautifully adorned Christmas tree on the planet.

After trying to corner his fiancée all evening, JJ trapped her in the dining room under the guise of helping her clear the dinner table. He suggested to the boys that they show Addy and her husband to the guest bedroom—the only other room Alex had insisted be furnished before the holiday—and take them on a tour of the house.

"JJ! They'll be back any minute," she gasped when he kissed a spot behind her ear.

"The boys will want to show them every nook and cranny. It should take a good fifteen minutes, at least." He tugged the dish towel from her and pitched it onto the counter, pulling her into the tight circle of his embrace. Cradling her head carefully, he bent closer and took her sweet sigh into his mouth. It was a long time before he lifted his head and then he did it only to sink his hands in the tumbling cloud of her hair for another kiss.

When he loosened his hold, Alex's mouth was glistening with his moisture and subtly swollen. Her fuzzy stare remained glued to his as she asked, "What was that for?"

"How about for giving me something I needed when I didn't even know I needed it?" He trailed his thumb over the dampness of her bottom lip. "No one's ever done anything like that for me before."

"So, you *really* don't mind that I contacted Addy?"

"I'm overjoyed, Alex, and it's not a feeling I've experienced a hell of a lot. Thank you." JJ was referring to more than just his gift, but the rest could wait until later.

"Merry Christmas, Jesse." Plucking a sprig of mistletoe from the table centerpiece, she tucked it behind his ear and instructed, "Kiss me again."

The dishes stayed dirty for a little while longer.

After the boys had reluctantly gone to bed, Alex thought about the jeep and went to move it into the garage. She'd scarcely buttoned her coat when JJ took the keys from her and volunteered to do it himself.

"But I'm dressed already. It'll just take a minute." She snatched the keys away from him, and he snatched them back. "I'm not fragile, JJ. The wind isn't strong enough to blow me over."

"The place is a mess, sweetheart. I was out there earlier." His blue-eyed gaze flitted past her and concentrated on some fascinating space over her shoulder.

"What's in there?" Alex suspiciously demanded.

"Where?"

"The garage."

He coughed. "Nothing."

"You got me something," she guessed, "and you didn't think I'd stumble on it out there."

"Maybe."

"I won't look, I swear. I'll park the jeep and come straight back."

"It's hard to miss," JJ hedged. "I couldn't wrap it up."

"Oh. You didn't have time."

"It would have taken up a bit, yes." He undid her coat and slipped her boots off. "You go relax with our guests. I'll see to the jeep."

"All right," she conceded and watched him go. It must be big if he couldn't wrap it. Perhaps he'd gotten that curio cabinet they'd seen at the mall . . . or the rocking chair in the antique shop. Whatever it was, she didn't care. He'd given her so much as it was. His warmth, his passion, a new home, security — everything but his love.

She resigned herself to the fact that while this wasn't an absolutely ideal situation, it was darned close. She'd been the one soured on marriage, so why did it bother her that he was sticking to the *arrangement*? Hadn't she known from the beginning that he wasn't the happy-ever-after type?

Alex brushed the sense of dissatisfaction aside. She'd take what she could get and be grateful she was the one he'd chosen to share his life with. After all, he was an ardent and considerate lover, a fine man to help raise her kids, and an extraordinary person in general. What more did she expect?

The Wentworths retired to their room shortly after JJ's return. They'd had a long trip and were worn out, so Addy hugged her hosts affectionately and preceded her husband up the stairs.

"Alone at last," JJ murmured as he reached for her.

Alex raised her mouth for his kiss and sighed contentedly. "This has been a perfect day. Mom and Dad will be by in the morning and then to dinner."

"Mmm. Are you sure you want to trust me with the turkey?"

"I'll supervise," she proposed. "I wonder if Elizabeth and Gerard will pop in. It'd be just like them to cause a scene." Bitterness rose in her, poisoning her restful mood.

"Oh God," JJ muttered, "I completely forgot. When you came in with Addy, it just flew right out of my head. Gerard called this afternoon."

Dread filled her as she waited for what she sensed would be a monumental moment. "About . . ."

JJ dipped his head. "The custody suit."

Alex sat on the edge of the sofa and held her breath for the announcement. Either way, she'd sacrifice her relationship with someone dear. That was the thought foremost in her mind. If the Mannings persisted in their bid for custody of Hank and Billy, she could possibly lose them. If they gave up, she'd lose the only man she'd ever truly loved.

Chapter Twelve

The pallor of Alex's face was intolerable, so he gave her the news directly. "They're not going ahead with it. Did you hear me?" he pressed when she only blinked at him. Joining her on the couch, JJ rubbed her cold hands briskly as he awaited a reaction.

"Just like that? It's over?" she whispered falteringly.

"Yeah, it's over." He longed to ask if that meant the end for them, too, but determined that it wasn't the right time. She deserved to bask in the comfort of knowing that her custody of the boys was not in jeopardy. His own selfish concerns could wait.

"What made them change their minds?" Alex queried in amazement. "Just a few days ago they were all set to drag me into court and lambaste my character."

"Well," JJ began, hoping she wouldn't be too angry that he hadn't told her of the information before now, "I had a little chat with Gerard. It seems that he and Elizabeth have been living beyond their means."

"That doesn't surprise me. Are they in debt up to their snooty noses?"

"No, they've managed to pay for the luxury cars, the condo in Gander, and Elizabeth's ridiculously expensive wardrobe."

Alex frowned perplexedly. "How?"

"With money that wasn't theirs to spend." JJ stood and paced the living room, shoving a big hand through his hair. He was going to have to tell her everything now. Not tomorrow or the next day — *now.* "I had Spike run a check on them for me. You know he can uncover just about anything, sometimes even before people who should already have an inkling about it get an inkling about it. Anyway, he wormed his way into Gerard's firm and got to the security office." He paused. "And the computer system."

"Is this all legal?"

"Mostly, but just in case . . ."

"Don't mention it to anyone." Alex gestured for him to continue.

"The bottom line is this. Elizabeth put him up to stealing money from the company accounts to help finance her preferred lifestyle, and Spike has both the video and the computer printouts to prove it. Plus, Elizabeth signed off on the bank deposits herself."

"So, she's an accessory." Confusion marred her face for a second, and he knew what the next question would be. "How long have you known about this?"

JJ looked away contritely. "Since the day we viewed the house."

"And when did you confront Gerard?"

"This past Monday." He fingered a bulb on the tree. She was upset, he could hear it in her voice. "I should have told you sooner, but I didn't know if threatening the Mannings with exposure would have the desired effect." Glad to be turned away from her so he didn't say the lie to her face, he compounded it with, "Also, I couldn't be sure Spike's information was one hundred percent accurate."

"Spike is always accurate."

"Yeah, usually."

"*Always*, JJ," she reiterated firmly. "You could have said something days ago and saved me a ton of worry."

There was nothing he could say to that. She was right. It had been selfish of him not to tell her the minute he'd found out, but he'd been consumed with keeping her close to him for just a little while longer.

"I thought we were going to be honest with each other." The disappointed tone tore at him mercilessly as she went on. "This doesn't bode well for a marriage, does it?"

"You're the expert on that, not me." Silence ticked on for what seemed like an eternity. He cleared his throat and faced her. "At any rate, this changes the reasons for our getting married. There's no custody battle looming on the horizon. Nobody's saying we have to go through with it." *Disagree with me, Alex, give me something to hang on to.* He held his breath until it burned in his chest, only venting it when the words he feared most were uttered.

"No, we don't have to." Her brown eyes were huge, and they glistened with unshed tears. "Hank and Billy will be crushed."

JJ swallowed hard, the last wisp of a dream life with her slipping away. Her sons would be distraught, but she'd get over it a lot faster—if there was anything in her heart to get over at all. "We don't need to tell them until after Christmas, Alex."

She shook her dark head mutely. Then, apparently satisfied that the subject was closed, rose from the couch and turned toward the stairs. "I'll bring down the presents before I go to bed."

"Do you want me to stay on the sofa tonight?" He didn't look her way but hid his expression so she didn't see the flicker of hope for one last night in her arms.

"No, the Wentworths will think it odd if they find you there."

So, they both put the gaily wrapped packages under the tree and turned out the lights, each footfall wearier than the last as they climbed the steps to their room.

Alex opted to take a quick shower and practically dove

for the bathroom, and JJ wondered if she was as relieved at this new turn of events as he'd assumed. *Of course she is, she's still clinging to the memory of her perfect husband.* The notion bugged him all over again, and when the water ran in the other room, something in him snapped. He needed to feel what it was like to make love with her just for one more night, to sink himself deep inside her and block out the world — past and present. He wanted to obliterate the picture she carried in her mind of her other lover, if only for a few hours, so that all she knew was him.

Dropping his clothes as he went, he strode to the bathroom and found her immersing her lush little body in the steaming cubicle. Sliding back the frosted door, he stepped inside and shut it deliberately behind him.

Loath to let him see how shaken and upset she was, Alex had fled to the shower to wallow in anguish privately. The tears flowed unchecked, and she tilted her face upward, the spray disguising all evidence of misery except the uncontrollable tremors that racked her body.

Even if he still wanted to get married, how could she rely on him to be open with her? He'd consciously kept her in the dark until the suit had been dropped. She was not a child who needed protecting or a harebrained idiot who couldn't run her own life. If the relationship didn't balance out all over, how was she supposed to trust him?

She knew he was there even before his hands slipped around her, the barely detectable draft from the door shutting hinting at his presence. He cupped her breasts and tipped them toward the pelting water when he curled his powerful body over hers, his erection boldly prodding the small of her back. The shower sluiced over his blond head when he leaned down to place a sizzling, open-mouthed kiss against her neck, plastering the hair to his scalp. She reached up to wrap an arm around him, desperately seeking a more secure hold. His hands rubbed her from shoulder to thigh and back and she arched wantonly against his hard shaft.

Suddenly, he turned her to face the wall and coaxed her to grip the stainless-steel rail. "Like this, Alex?" he rasped in her ear. "Do you want me like this?"

The ability to speak was lost to her, so she nodded once and braced herself for his entry. He positioned her legs readily, both arms enfolding her possessively, his mouth latching on to the tender flesh of her shoulder. At the same time that he suckled strongly on her skin, he penetrated her slick heat in one glorious, eager thrust, nearly lifting her off the floor. It exhilarated Alex beyond reason, and she was powerless to do anything but close her eyes tightly and meet his strokes while he pounded into her. Again and again he drove her to climax until, finally, he lowered them both to their knees and cushioned her cautiously while he found his own release, hoarsely calling her name as he filled her.

Collapsing backward into his embrace, Alex vaguely perceived that the water had cooled a fraction and was about to get cooler. She stretched a limp hand to the wash cloth she'd discarded on the tiles and worked a lather into it. Turning carefully, she soaped JJ's exquisitely proportioned body wherever she could reach, gingerly grazing the most intimate part of him. When the water had chased away the suds, he took the cloth and did the same for her, stopping to place gentle kisses on her upturned face.

The shower was almost frigid when JJ shut it off. Retrieving a thick towel from just outside the cubicle, he dried her briskly, restoring warmth to chilled bones. Her hair had to be wrung to get the water out before he scrubbed it in another towel and then efficiently wiped himself dry.

Alex watched him hungrily, wondering if this would be

the last time for them. Simply being lovers after all they'd planned together would pale in comparison. She went to him again and kissed him longingly, attempting to communicate without words how badly she wanted him, wanted his love, despite her uneasiness with his habit of not confiding everything.

JJ picked her up and walked back to the bedroom, gently setting her in the middle of their bed. He tucked the comforter around her and soundlessly returned to the other room, emerging a moment later with a hair dryer in one hand. Completely at ease with his nudity—for which she was extremely grateful—he located an outlet near the bed and plugged it in. Then, kneeling on the wide mattress, he pulled Alex into a sitting position and fanned her curly tresses with warm air. Tipping her head this way and that, she kept her eyes locked on his until the task was accomplished thoroughly.

When he would have turned off the dryer, she claimed it and held it to his damp hair, ruffling the light strands with her fingers. He laughed huskily as she trained the nozzle on his chest and did the same. Pushing him down so that he lay across her lap, Alex followed a narrowing path over the flat plane of his stomach and lower, to the region where his excitement was rapidly gaining prominence once more. She killed the hair dryer and flung it away, nearly breaking it when it thumped to the floor.

JJ chuckled slyly. "In a hurry to get somewhere?"

"Yes. Come up here," she ordered, prim, "and lay next to me."

"What will you give me?"

Alex growled, so he did as he was told. She thoughtfully covered him to the waist and brushed her mouth across his nipples. He lay pliantly, and she hovered above his lips, whispering with heat, "I'll give you something to remember me by," and proceeded to make her way down his body.

"Baby, you don't have to . . ." He gasped at the first touch of her mouth.

"Shut up, Jesse," was her soft suggestion, and she flicked her tongue along the sensitive underside of him, his muscles jerking reflexively. He held himself rigid after that, allowing her to taste the only part of him she hadn't when they'd made love before.

Alex knew she was driving him crazy, felt the frantic desire emanating from his moist skin. Pausing in her erotic assault, she shifted and raised up on her knees, drawing his heavy thighs over hers while she lowered her mouth and took him inside, pulling wetly on him until he cursed raggedly and begged her to stop. She complied, straddling his undulating hips quickly and savoring the sensation of having him explode into her with one soul-shattering thrust.

JJ lay staring at the ceiling in the dark and fondled a silken curl absently. Alex had cuddled into his side, her cheek pressed close to his heart. He knew she was still awake by the sound of her uneven breathing—he'd spent hours in the brief time they'd been intimate just listening to the serene cadence of her respiration as she'd slept in his arms. She was definitely not sleepy now. Her hand moved restively on his chest, smoothing the coarse hair slowly. A sigh feathered his skin, the sound scarcely heard above the raggedness of his own.

Scalding hot liquid spilled from his eyes, streaming heedlessly down his face and onto the pillow. Was this how it was going to end? Would the morning come soon and erase the passion, the warmth and love from his life? Would she avoid his presence as much as possible at the office and altogether outside of it? And could he stand seeing her every day, damning himself for telling her that the suit had been dropped before they'd gone through with the wedding?

What of his relationship with the boys? The feelings he had for Hank and Billy could no easier be ignored or extinguished than those he felt for their mother.

Another desolate breath vibrated in his chest. Maybe he and Alex could remain lovers and he'd still be an active participant in all their lives — at least until she fell in love with someone. After all, she couldn't stay tied to a ghost forever, could she? How long before a man like Darryl came along and wanted her for his wife, leaving JJ where he'd always ended up, on the outside looking in?

"I love you, Alex." The tormented whisper seemed to rip itself from his mouth, escaping into the tense silence of the room unexpectedly. "Damn, I didn't mean to say that."

"Didn't mean to say it or didn't *mean* it?" She propped herself up on his chest, and he was stunned to realize that her face was as wet as his. "Well?"

"I love you," he blurted again.

"Then why did we just make love like it was the last time? If you love me, JJ, why do you want me to leave?"

"Because I know you don't feel the same."

Puzzlement was written all over her tear-stained face. "You don't know anything."

"No?" He scrubbed at his eyes in frustration, trying not to embarrass himself any further. Here he was, a grown man, practically blubbering over a woman. It was absurd. "You want me, Alex, care for me even. I know that. But I'll never measure up to what you had before."

"What are you going on about?" she muttered, obviously trying to keep her voice down.

"Darryl. Remember him?"

"How could I forget?"

JJ flinched at that. "You're still in love with him."

In the dim lamplight, he could see her eyes enlarging until they resembled extravagant pools of chocolate. "Why would you think that? I've never said anything to that effect, have I?"

Her confounded frown took him aback. "You said you never wanted to marry again, that you didn't want to rely on another person because they'd—"

"JJ," she interrupted tiredly, "I meant Darryl let me down. Not because he died and left me alone, but because I believed in him and gave him everything I had, only to find that he'd been careless and unfaithful." Moving to his side, Alex lay on the pillow and peered closely at him. "I was infatuated with the idea of being in love and naïve enough to believe Darryl's promises. If I hadn't thought this was just a marriage of convenience for you . . . well, I'd have explained my attitude sooner. I really didn't think my first run at holy matrimony was relevant."

"He cheated on you?" JJ was angry when he imagined how hurt she must have been to find out.

"I honestly didn't intend to make him out to be some paragon of virtue—he wasn't. In fact, he had more than one fault, and ultimately I ended up paying for it." Alex touched her nose to his. "You are so different from him. I kept wondering when you'd wake up and discover you were too good for me."

"Alex," he said roughly, attempting to erase the shadows from her eyes. "I adore you. That's simply the way it is. You've had me knocked for a loop ever since we met. How could you not see it? My God, the reason I didn't tell you about the information Spike had compiled was that I wanted just a few more measly days with you."

"You didn't keep it from me for any other reason? Not even some misguided attempt to take care of my problems?" Earnestly, she insisted, "I'm a big girl, JJ, and I need to be treated as an equal."

"Is that how it was in your marriage, or am I getting a hint here?" He figured there was an underlying cause to her being so bothered that he'd failed to tell her about the Mannings.

"My marriage was very lopsided in some ways. Darryl kept too much from me. It's a long story, but—do you really love me?" she asked in wonder, switching the subject again. "You're not just saying that because it's what I want to hear?"

He leaned over and solemnly confirmed, "I have only said those words to you and the boys. I'll say it as often as it takes for you to believe it. If you give me the chance, I'll tell you every single day for the rest of my life—countless times, I swear." Taking her in his arms, he kissed her deeply and for a long time. "Will you tell me about Darryl?" he asked quietly.

Alex spoke against his mouth, haltingly at first. "I discovered he was gambling. A lot. I mean, he'd drained the bank accounts, maxed out the credit cards, everything."

"Gerard mentioned something about his spending habits."

"Mmm-hmm. Well, he wasn't buying anything tangible, not for me and the kids, anyway. I have some idea when he started seeing his mistress. It was around the time I became pregnant with Billy, I think. He rarely touched me after that—he complained that it was my fault, that I was frigid and blamed him for the mess our finances were in. I didn't, really, but once I found out about his girlfriend and that he was still gambling, I left.

"Then, he was diagnosed with cancer, and I went back to take care of him. I no longer fooled myself that there was a marriage to salvage, but he needed somebody, and his parents were hopeless. He was the boys' father, even if he'd never had much interest in them." She caressed his cheek thoughtfully. "You're their dad, the only one they've really ever known, and they love you. I love you, too."

JJ inhaled deeply and kissed her palm. "Say it again."

She did, whispering the words over and over as he stared into her dark eyes and let them invade his very being, chasing out the demons of the past and ushering in light and new hope for the future.

"I promise you, Alex, I'll never keep anything from you again. This relationship thing is new for me," he told her honestly. "I hope you'll have some patience. I'll be a willing student if you'll teach me a little."

"I'd like nothing better." Her smile was beautiful.

They talked a while longer, answering each other's questions and putting fears to rest. The wedding would happen as planned, but the bride and groom would truly be pledging their love and not entering into an advantageous *arrangement*.

"I think this is fast becoming my favorite time of year," JJ told her right before they fell asleep. "I'm getting everything I wished for."

"What Santa can't bring, I'll find for you." Alex brushed her lips over his. "Always, Jesse. Merry Christmas."

"Merry Christmas, darling." A sense of peace stole over him as he closed his eyes, knowing she'd be there in the morning and every morning after.

Epilogue

One year later

Alex slid a hand over the slight swell of her belly and smiled softly. Just another four months, and she and JJ would welcome their child into the world.

At times like this, she fought the urge to pinch herself to be sure she wasn't dreaming. Her sons were on the floor with their father, frowns of concentration marring their brows as the three of them attempted to figure out how to put the new telescope together. It was a Christmas gift from Addy and Albert, who had moved back to St. John's and were an important part of the family.

George and Lorna were enjoying their vacation in PEI and had called to wish them all a Merry Christmas, promising to be home in time to celebrate Alex and JJ's anniversary.

From the door to the kitchen, she looked at her husband and silently thanked God that he'd come into their lives. He was wonderful with Hank and Billy, so loving and patient. He'd been absolutely flabbergasted to learn that they were pregnant. Alex had thoroughly relished the way he'd gaped at her and then stuttered incoherently. She adored him with every fiber of her being and told him so regularly, thrilling at the light in his eyes when he responded in kind.

JJ had made good on his promise to help with the children while she finished her degree, babysitting and keeping up with his half of the housework without having to be reminded. He'd shocked her with the purchase of a minivan last year, showing her exactly how sincere he was about ensuring her independence. Alex thought he was a gem.

Their passion for each other hadn't cooled one bit either, she mused. With every day they shared as husband and wife, the profound sense of intimacy between them reached a greater depth.

Life was virtually perfect—except she still caught him putting the empty milk carton back in the fridge every now and then. She had to excuse at least one bad habit, didn't she? Besides, the rewards far exceeded the troubles they'd run into since getting married. They did spar occasionally, but neither was too stubborn to ignore the merits of the other's argument, and JJ claimed he was grateful that she helped keep him sharp.

All in all, everyone was happy.

"What's on your mind, Mrs. Vanzant?" JJ nudged her backward into the relative privacy of the kitchen.

"You. Us." She kissed him tenderly, placing his warm hands on the growing mound of her stomach. "I love you."

He grinned and pressed his forehead to hers. "Music to my ears. Is there anything I can get you? Something to eat, a back rub?"

"You give me everything I'll ever need or want. There's just one thing . . ."

"Mmm?"

"A little girl?" she murmured.

"Oh, I promise you," he said soberly, "if this baby isn't female, we'll definitely keep trying!"

You may also enjoy the following from eXtasy Books Inc:

That Pushy Kincaid
Quinn K Clancy and Mary Clancy

Excerpt

Mornings were Meg's favorite time of day. She loved to see the first rays of sun filtering through the curtains as she looked out the window at the waking world, a cup of herbal tea in her hand.

This morning she'd slept in later than usual due to her bout with insomnia and had risen to stumble to the shower, clumsily shedding her pajamas as she went. The warm spray had restored her senses somewhat, making the task of dressing in baggy jeans and denim shirt less complicated than she'd feared. Even knotting her shirttails together hadn't posed a major problem.

Her red ringlets still damp, she trudged barefoot to the kitchen and filled the kettle, setting it to boil while she leaned against the counter and surveyed her new home.

The old house was roomy by anyone's standards, even someone who'd spent eighteen years of her life in the lap of luxury. The kitchen was large and airy, its wooden cabinets and yellow walls cheery. Her bedroom was the ideal size for her old brass bed, two dressers, and a vanity. The bathroom had been modernized to include a shower stall as well as the claw-footed tub. A spacious living room opened off the kitchen and currently contained an ivory-colored sofa and matching chair to complement the old-fashioned shiplap paneling on the walls. The dining room was small, but she'd decided that would serve as part of her work space along with the spare bedroom.

All of her things had been stored and arranged to her satisfaction after two days of lugging and unpacking. Her friends had been more than accommodating, a fact for which she was extremely grateful.

The kettle whistled, snapping her out of her reverie. She sighed at the first sip of hot tea and wandered to the window. The sight that greeted her there was more than a little strange. Steven Kincaid was half stooped over the bonnet of his car, one hand on his behind and the other waving at three boys who were apparently blowing raspberries and dodging capture excitedly. Meg frowned when she realized the man was unable to move from his uncomfortable semi-crouch and was becoming more annoyed and harried by the second. She left her tea on the counter and went to investigate.

"Excuse me," Meg called from the top of the steps, shielding her eyes from the bright sun. "Is something wrong, Mr. Kincaid?"

The three boys scampered away at the sound of her voice, chuckling gleefully all the way down the street.

One thick, dark brow arched as the tall man scowled over his shoulder at her. "I'm attached to my car." His face and ears turned red with humiliation.

Meg, still in her bare feet, left the porch to stand beside him. He turned his gaze straight ahead, and a pang of sympathy twanged inside her when she noticed that he was, indeed, tied to his car. "How did you manage that?"

"Does it matter?" he mildly enquired, a vein in his neck

prominently indicating his stress. "My tie got stuck, and the door locked on its own."

"Mmm. I can see." She peered more closely at his flushed face. He really was a handsome man, and very embarrassed. "What do you want me to do? Get your spare keys?"

"They're in my briefcase. In my apartment."

"Ah. Do you have a cell phone — or is that in your briefcase, too?"

"No, my cell phone is in my car." Then he added, "The tie was a gift from my niece — otherwise I'd just get you to cut it."

Meg looked through the windshield and sighed. "Can I call someone from my place?"

"Oh, would you?" was the sarcastic response.

"Maybe."

Heaving those wide shoulders, he bowed his head and mumbled, "Please. I can't stoop any lower to loosen and unknot the damn thing. My face hits the bonnet."

"What's the number?" she relented. The poor man had suffered enough at the hands of those rude kids. There was no reason for her to act like a juvenile.

The car's hostage rattled off a number and told her who to ask for. "Tell him I need him to jimmy open my door. ASAP!"

Meg jogged back inside and placed the call. On the second ring, a pleasant female voice said, "Hello."

"Hi, could I speak with JJ? It's rather urgent."

"One minute, I'll catch him before he gets in his car." The phone was dropped abruptly, and a few moments passed. Meg waited for the woman to come back. "Sorry about that. Here he is now." A low conversation took place while the receiver was transferred from one hand to another.

"Vanzant," a deep baritone rumbled tersely.

"Hello. I'm calling for Steven Kincaid." Meg quickly explained what had happened and conveyed the request for her neighbor's expeditious release.

"Stevie got his tie jammed in the door?" Laughter roared across the line as the man grasped the ridiculous situation. "I'll be right there."

Biting her quivering lip, she informed the bent prisoner that help was on the way. She couldn't resist an interested peek at his tight bottom when he leaned against the car. Poor, poor, sexy man. He was really embarrassed.

"I have another problem and I don't think it'll wait for JJ to get here." A pregnant pause followed his announcement. "I have to use the bathroom."

"Oh. Oh my." Grabbing her sides to stop the giggles from erupting, she ignored his strident objections and bolted for her apartment. Once hidden from view, she doubled over and laughed until tears streamed down her face. She had to do something. The man had to go, and she couldn't let him languish in the driveway while she stayed inside.

He didn't protest when he saw her coming with the scissors. In fact, the look of pure relief on his face said that he welcomed any solution wholeheartedly, even one that destroyed his coveted gift.

Meg carefully reached around him and cut the silky material in two, bracing his cramped frame as he straightened despite the heat that raced through her at the feel of his hard body. How strange that other men seemed to hold their warmth much easier than he did. Steven Kincaid radiated like a furnace.

"Thank you," he threw over one shoulder and ran for the front door, in a hurry to relieve himself. He stopped suddenly at the foot of the steps.

"Just go in and use my bathroom," Meg offered, seeing the fix he was in. He had no keys to open his apartment with, after all. She trailed behind him slowly, trying desperately to restrain her mirth.

Steven washed his hands and stared glumly at the rumpled, flustered image that was his reflection. He'd never been so utterly humiliated in front of a beautiful woman — a stunning, flame-haired, long-legged paragon of sensuality with the bluest eyes he'd ever seen. When he'd raised his head to find her walking toward him in that languid way she had of moving, he decided he didn't give a damn if she was a hippie or a nun. She'd knocked the wind out of him.

The Voice had ceased to exist. Now, he thought of her as simply . . . The Vision.

Rapidly drying his hands, he grinned ruefully at the triangle of blue fabric that hung pathetically below his tie knot. She was inventive. Cute. Taken.

There were no signs of her male companion in the bathroom. Only feminine soaps and makeup, moisturizers, and shampoo littered the counter next to the sink. That meant nothing except that her lover didn't live with her — yet.

Maybe the guy was still lounging in bed. He'd been in too much of a hurry to relieve himself to notice if the bedroom door was shut.

Steven let loose a four-letter word and warily exited the bathroom, checking left and right before treading down the hall to the kitchen. There, calmly sipping from a mug, was The Vision. Her enormous blue eyes danced merrily as she sized him up.

"Feeling better?" she queried.

"Much." He cleared his throat. "I hope I didn't take you away from, ah, anything."

Frowning slightly, she said, "No. There's coffee if you'd like to wait for your friend here. I'm afraid all I have is instant."

He glanced furtively around but saw no evidence of her fellow squeaker. "No, thanks. JJ shouldn't be much longer. I'll just go back out to the car."

"Okay." The Vision narrowed her splendid eyes, thick lashes obscuring her expression. "By the way, what were those kids doing earlier?"

"Polishing their criminal techniques. Johnny and the gang are sort of a suburban mini-mob," he explained and headed for the door. "Bye."

"See ya."

Outside, Steven chastised himself for not thanking her properly. He'd make it up to her somehow. Right now, he had a big, blond PI to deal with who happened to be grinning broadly as he trained a cell phone on what was left of his buddy's tie.

"This is one for the books, Stevie." JJ snapped a picture and turned to the car. He clicked another shot of the material fluttering from the door. "I'll make duplicates for everyone we know."

"Shut up, Vanzant."

The blond PI couldn't stop one last wicked chuckle before unlocking the car.

About the Authors

Quinn and Mary Clancy are two sisters who have been writing romance for several years. Quinn is a published author but this is Mary's first books. Originally, the Triple Threat series was written in the late 90's and has been updated by the two for publication. Her Protector is the first book of the series.